Firewalker

THE COLEMANS' LEGACY BOOK 1

JAMIE BEGLEY

Young Ink Press Publication
YoungInkPress.com

Edited by CD Editing, Erin Toland,
& Diamond in the Rough Editing
Cover Art by Cover Couture

Connect with Jamie,
Facebook.com/AuthorJamieBegley
Instagram.com/authorjamiebegley
JamieBegley.net

Preface

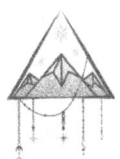

Their names were forgotten, erased from existence, becoming just another Native American couple torn from their native land. The woman carried in her womb the gifts given by the gods, in repayment for defending the Mother of Creation. The gifts were to be bestowed on their children and the future generations to come.

As their days grew dark with their struggles to survive along the perilous journey to their new homeland, the gods watched their courage, yet never once did they try to take advantage of the stone the man carried within his chest to lessen their hardships.

Decades later, they were buried side by side on the land they had worked tirelessly on to leave a lasting legacy to their children. The secret had been sworn on and died with them, and the threat to humanity lost for all time. Mankind would never know of how close they had come to extinction, nor of the sacrifices made by the man and woman who died protecting the secret.

Fate was given the duty to watch over their children, care-fully monitoring how the gifts were used by the couple's progeny. As new generations were born, Fate came to Mother in concern that their gifts made other humans fearful of them and were seeking to destroy what could not be understood in the human realm. Mother began watching them herself to see what consequences the gifts had wrought, making adjustments when needed. She might have created Earth, but it was still a work in progress.

From Hades, they had been given the gift to create and manipulate fire and to astral project themselves through the Shadow realm of time. Wisely, Mother had deemed this gift too powerful for one mortal to hold, splitting the gift into two. One to be given the power of light, the other of the shadow realm, capable of walking between Earth and Heaven. Both must be born at the same time, for light must keep darkness from consuming the shadow realm.

When their progeny nearly died out from disease, Mother called on Zephyrus to bestow his gift of wind on a descendent. Fire cannot breathe without air.

Rocque, the Lord of the Forests, had been given the gift of controlling nature. Mother watched those who welded that power closely, as the gift almost rivaled her own power over Earth. Jealous, she decided to finetune that gift, limiting the recipients of that particular power of Earth, only allowing them to wield it within their own domain, and able to shelter and protect those they love within the boundaries of the mountain they called home.

When one unexpected gift came to light, Mother could only shake her head. Her son, Poseidon, had snuck the power of water on the woman, as a reward for protecting the stone. Water can give life or take it away with a fury that could mimic her own when she was angry.

Shaking her head in amusement at some of the progenies' misdeeds, Mother didn't let her growing affection for the family sway their punishment when Asclepius' gift was misused by one of the female descendants, by saving a life meant to be taken. Sadly, Mother had Fate intervene to break the family line in two different directions. The repercussion was severe in which any of the descendants gifted with the healing arts were separated from the main trunk of gifts, which were becoming more powerful each generation.

While she didn't regret separating the family into two branches, she felt sorrow witnessing the cruel hardships the new branch had to endure. Wanting to prevent such a harsh punishment in the future, she gave them her last gift.

She had taken Astraios' gifts away as punishment for fighting with Chronos. Mother bestowed his powers which she had carefully hoarded to herself, giving the progenies the ability to read the stars and the skies, allowing them to read the paths laid out for them to follow. It was a huge gift, which would come with severe penalties if they misused it.

To make sure no family member overstepped their boundaries again, she decided there would be a safeguard born into each generation, which would have the ability to harness all the powers gifted to them. They would be her failsafe. They would carry their knowledge and the cost of their powers to the next generation. They would teach and prepare those who would follow in their footsteps. Lessons which would warn them from abusing their gifts. Their powers were gifts and weren't to be profited from and never, ever to seek to try to usurp Her power again.

Continuing to monitor the family intermittently, despite having given Fate the duty, she watched both branches of the family grow in numbers until one particular soul was born.

A male child with all the gifts.

Mother wasn't ashamed to admit she grew fond of the mortal, yet despite her fondness, she wasn't able to change the future laid out before him in the stars. He would never find his soul mate during the lifetime he had been born into. The star-crossed lovers kept missing each other, their love destined for another lifetime.

Used to philandering males, Mother watched in amusement as her favored one didn't let a lack of a soul mate deter him from finding another way to share the love he was capable of by creating life after life. He even extended his love to an outsider. Loving each child with a pure heart, he taught his children the power of their gifts with a reference she hadn't felt in eons.

When he begot a female child that had a healing power, she cried just as hard as her father when he read the stars, showing her future. The child would become too powerful to allow to remain in their branch of the family. Not only had she been born with a healing gift bequeathed from a god, also inheriting the healing touch from their native ancestors which only one other could brag about, but like all mothers, she couldn't leave well enough alone, making the soul stronger by being able to use energy derived from nature to restore her strength.

The soul needed to be switched to the other branch of the family, where they had learned the cost of using their gifts unwisely.

Her affection for the family held her hand at removing the female child until her father was given a chance to beget the child who would one day step into his shoes.

Then, with an aching heart, she called them both to Heaven together. However, they weren't together long before the female soul was sent back to Earth. Mother made certain this time that the gifted soul would be protected by a fierce warrior and a mother who loved and appreciated the nature around her. Just as important, she would be guided by a family member who would teach her how to use the gift, tempered by the personal costs she would ultimately pay throughout her lifetime.

Mother watched the offspring left on Earth with a careful eye, seeing the same qualities and commitments to those they loved as the ancestors who had fought for her in her greatest time of need.

Finally, her patience and planning were about to come to fruition. The eight brothers had the powers of demigods, the stars were aligned to where she needed them and, crucial to her plans, they had the strength of will and courage to protect the *rewards* she was about to give them. The culmination of her plan hinged on their ability to convince their *rewards* to love them.

Love was the only variable out of her control. They would have to earn the love on their own without her help or Valentine's gift.

Yes, it was frustrating for her ... So many variables could go wrong ... She had made so many promises. Mankind's fate was on the line yet again—there was a battle looming on the horizon, and those eight demigods were the only way to bring order back to the mortal, and the immortal realm. She was now at the hardest part of being Mother. All she could do was watch and trust her demigods prove their valance. It would hurt her deeply if they failed, because she was at an impasse. She couldn't interfere, despite all her immense power, held in the palm of her hand. It all hinged on the most basic of human emotions ...

Love.

Prologue

S he could hear the monster coming.

Alanna shuffled to the side to hide behind the curtain, praying she wouldn't be found in the dark room. Dread filled her with each step she could hear outside in the hallway.

"Please, don't come in here ... Please, God," she prayed silently to herself, the prayer freezing in her mind when she heard the sound of the doorknob being turned. Terror held her mind and body paralyzed, as if she were in some Matrix glitch, waiting for what would happen next while knowing she had played this game too many times not to know the penalty of being the loser.

Holding her breath, hearing soft footsteps enter the room, Alanna was so lost in terror that she nearly wet herself when the footsteps stopped near her, so close she could hear the monster's intake of breath.

"I know you're in here, Alanna. Come out, and I'll let you pick the movie we'll watch. If not ..."

The threat hung in the air, waiting for a response from her, which Alanna had no intention of giving.

She remained frozen in place, even after the footsteps had started moving around the room again and the monster had slammed the closet door open to search inside. She had known the monster would come out tonight.

Today was her birthday, and the monster came out to play anytime any joy could filter into her life.

The closing of the closet door had Alanna bracing to be found again as the footsteps were on the move again.

"I'm going to let you win tonight, Alanna, because it's your birthday."

Alanna didn't believe the monster's lies. She had been taken in too many times before.

"I had a special present I was going to give you. I guess you'll never know what it is."

She didn't care what it was.

Voices coming up the steps had the monster moving to the door.

"You win, but I can't let you go unpunished. You're going to get it twice as bad the next time we play. I don't leave for a couple of more nights, so I'll make sure we'll spend plenty of quality time together before then."

The barely-heard click of the door closing behind the monster had her legs collapsing out from under her. Shoving a fist against her mouth, she managed to stifle the cries coming from her throat so her foster parents wouldn't hear as they walked past her bedroom and came inside to see why she was crying.

She just had to make it a couple more nights, and then the monster would be gone.

Too afraid the monster would come back when the Fields went to sleep, she remained in the same spot until she felt the sun's rays burning the side of her face. As she lifted her face to the bright sun, the terror of the night melted under the warmth.

The Fields usually kept the house chilly, to keep her foster mother comfortable. Alanna was used to feeling the chill, despite wearing a warm robe over her clothes.

Raising her hand, she pressed it against the pane of the glass, feeling the warmth heat her palm. Lingering instead of getting dressed, she wished the next two days would magically pass her by.

When she heard the other children stirring to get ready for school, Alanna stiffly got to her feet, dropping her hand to her side when a brisk knock sounded on her door.

"You up, Alanna?" Mrs. Field's asked. "Hurry up, or you won't have time to eat breakfast."

"I'll hurry."

"I made French toast. You better hurry, or there won't be any left," she called out, her voice moving farther away.

Even though she was no longer touching the pane of glass, the chill settled back into her bones. There was no magic left in the world strong enough to make the coming days pass quickly. At fourteen, she was too old to still believe in magic. Her life was no fairy tale, and she wasn't a princess, nor would any prince be coming to her rescue.

After hurriedly dressing, Alanna was tugging on her shoes when the door opened without warning.

She fearfully glanced at the doorway to see an older girl, who didn't share the same lack of confidence, saunter inside. If anyone considered herself royalty, it was the teenager who was looking at her in irritation.

"Why aren't you ready yet?"

Staring at the angelic blonde who could be a Victoria Secret model with an inferiority complex, Alanna jumped off the bed to shrug on her backpack. "I'm ready."

Irritated, Kate put on a sweet smile, as if she were royalty bestowing a reward on a peasant. "Good. I'd hate for you to miss out on French toast." She gave an encouraging wave of her hand to motion for her to go first.

Alanna started to move past Kate to head to the door when Kate flashed out a fist. Alanna didn't have time to react, other than to drop to her knees as the air was knocked out of her lungs.

She was still trying to catch her breath when Kate sauntered back to the open doorway to close the door. Shutting them both inside before returning to her side, Kate buried a hand in her hair to drag her head backward.

"Our games aren't any fun for me if I can't find you.", she snarled.

"We'll be late for school," Alanna gasped out, not trying to twist away from her sister's touch.

"I won't be. Jackson is picking me up to drive me." Kate twisted her hair tighter in her grip. "Where did you hide your birthday money?"

"I didn't. I asked Mrs. Fields to keep it for me."

Kate cruelly arched Alanna's neck farther back. "Then you better get it back before I get out of school."

Alanna knew the pain she would be made to experience would be worse than the money was worth.

"I will."

Shoving her aside, Kate went to the door. "Jeez, you're such a slow poke. Come on." Kate opened the door. "If you're done eating by the time Jackson gets here, I'll let you ride with us."

She would rather walk the three miles to school than ride with the high school couple, but she forced a grateful smile to her lips. "Thanks, Kate."

Kate slung an arm around her shoulders, yet her sisterly expression and tone of voice didn't match the cold gaze that stared down at her. "I'll always take care of my little sister, even when I *have* to move away. Don't forget that."

"I won't." A chill raced down her back when a muscled teenager filled the doorway, blocking them.

"You get it?"

"Not yet. She gave it to Bev. She'll have it by the time we get home from school." Kate's hold on Alanna's shoulder became a stranglehold around her neck as they both watched in amusement at her gasping for air. "Isn't that right, sis?"

"Yes," she managed to gasp out.

Kate's hold around her neck immediately loosened. "See? I told you I have it under control."

"You better," he warned. "I don't want to be disappointed like I was last night."

"I made it up to you, didn't I?" Kate cooed. "Let's go eat before Bev comes up here to see what's taking so long."

A smile crossed her foster brother's lips that always turned her stomach into knots, and Owen didn't move away from the doorway.

"Why should if I care if the stupid bitch comes up here? She's going to kick us out of here in a couple of days, anyway. What's a couple of days going to matter?"

A sigh of impatience came from Kate. "I've told you before why we don't want to cause trouble. Play smart, and you never get caught. Stupidity will get you caught every time. It's why you were in four different foster homes before you met me. Now, move. I'm hungry."

Owen moved aside, but not before giving Alanna a promissory look. "When I get home, you better have my money," he threatened.

His money?

Too frightened and timid to assert herself, Alanna could only give him a fearful nod. Owen's bullying behavior had been gradually worsening the closer he was to aging out of the system. The last couple of days, she had practically been quaking in her shoes every time she heard him in the house, terrified of what he would do.

"I'll ask for it back."

Owen didn't appear appeased by her assurance, but at least he lost the scary look, which was habitually on his face when he looked at her.

She meekly walked alongside them to go downstairs while her stomach churned, expecting at any second for Owen to jerk her into any of the rooms they had to pass.

When they entered the kitchen, Mrs. Fields turned from doing the dishes, taking in their expressions as they took their chairs. She fixed them a plate then turned back to her dishes, so she missed Owen taking two of her French toast sticks, leaving her with only one.

She slowly ate the small amount of food left for her without speaking up and telling on the much older teen. And, not wanting to ride to school with Kate, she ignored the kicks under the table for her to hurry up and gripped her fork tighter at the sudden blare of a car horn from outside.

"Let's go, Alanna." Kate stood up from the table expectantly.

Mrs. Fields turned from the sink. "Go ahead, Kate." Moving to the stove, her foster mother carried a platter of French toast to the table to place three more on Alanna's plate. "I'm sure Owen wouldn't mind a ride to school; it'll save him from being late again."

Unfazed by the heated glare Owen turned on her, Mrs. Fields gave him a stony glance, showing him she was unmoved by his bullying behavior. "Unless you get your diploma, you won't qualify for the transition housing your caseworker found for you."

Alanna could see Owen biting back what he wanted to say. Instead, he jerked himself to his feet and carried his dirty dishes to the sink.

Kate jumped to her feet at the sound of the dishes crashing inside the sink.

Scarfing down the food once Kate and Owen had left, Alanna started to rise from the table with her empty plate in hand.

"There's no need to rush." Mrs. Fields gave her a gentle smile. "Your caseworker is coming by for a visit. She wants to have a chat with you."

Feeling the color drain from her cheeks, she shakily sat back down. "You're sending me back to the group home?"

Mrs. Fields covered her trembling hand with hers. "Only for a few days, until Kate and Owen leave."

"I don't understand." Alanna stared at the older woman in confusion.

"I've been taking care of children in my home long enough to know when something isn't right. I can see you becoming more terrified of Kate and Owen every day, so I think it's best if you move to a group home until they are moved into their new housing."

Alanna didn't know whether to be relieved or become more frightened. Even when they moved out, they would still know where to find her when she returned to Mrs. Fields's house, which school she went to. They were going to be furious about the birthday money, and not having someone to do their bidding when she was unfortunate enough to be around them. They knew she was afraid of them, and they wouldn't give up without a fight. They fed on her terror, so they would starve until they found someone new to take advantage of. And when they went hungry, no one was safe.

Mrs. Fields gave her a discerning look. "If you don't want to come back, I understand. That's another reason your case-worker is coming. She can find another foster family where they'll have a hard time finding you."

"I don't want another home." Blinking back tears of fright, Alanna stared at her foster mother imploringly.

"I don't want you, too, either. I've decided not to take in any more foster children. You'll be the only one here, other than Sam. You and Sam get along okay, don't you?"

"Yes." She sniffled. "I like Sam."

"I'm kind of partial to him myself. Of course, he's my son, so I could be biased. With you and Sam to take care of, I'll be able to take you back and forth to your appointments, and you won't have to ride the bus anymore. You can go outside and sit on the back porch; think about it until your caseworker arrives."

"Yes, ma'am."

Taking her dishes to the sink, Alanna started to head out the back door, but paused. Unable to hold back her happiness, she returned to the table to hug Mrs. Fields.

"Thank you. I like living here."

"I like having you here, too," Mrs. Fields returned gruffly. "Scoot. I hear a car in the driveway. I need a few minutes with your caseworker."

Nodding, Alanna practically skipped out the back door to take a seat on the swing.

As she stared out at the overgrown lawn, she promised herself she would learn how to work the lawnmower, which gave Mrs. Fields such fits in her back each time she had to use it. Owen had refused to mow the grass each time he was asked. She also promised to do all the chores Kate hadn't helped with.

Without Owen and Kate in the house and not having to see them again, it felt as if a whole new life was opening up to her. One where she wouldn't have to be so afraid.

She bit her bottom lip as her happiness dimmed. No matter how much Mrs. Fields would try to protect her, she had a sinking feeling in her stomach that Kate and Owen would just be waiting to strike when she least expected it.

"Should I not come back?" she mused out loud to herself. The last time she had left a foster home, she was stuck in a group home for thirteen months before Mrs. Fields accepted her as a placement.

There was nothing about her that drew the attention of prospective foster parents. She was too young to do many of the chores that would make life easier for those who wanted to foster. When she had been younger, she lived in several foster homes, and was shuffled out the door each time her foster parents found themselves expecting a child of their own.

"I don't want to go to another home," she mused out loud again. Mrs. Fields always made sure she had enough to eat and changed her bed as much as she did Sam's. One of the biggest reasons that she didn't want to leave was Sam. Despite the five-year age gap, she had grown closer to him while she and Kate had grown further apart. Both Owen and Kate were smart enough to keep their hands to themselves where Sam was concerned. Since he was Mrs. Fields's natural son, they didn't want to chance being thrown out by her. As far as foster homes went, Mrs. Fields's was the best any of them had ever lived in.

"They'll know where to find you." Alanna knew Kate would never let her slip out of her grasp. On the other hand, did she want to chance being placed in a foster home where someone worse than Kate and Owen lived?

"I'm scared. I don't know what to do."

The leaves on the tree next to the porch started waving on the branches as a calming breeze gently blew through them.

"*Stay. Grow stronger. I'll tell you when to run.*"

Alanna didn't blink at the wind talking to her. It was just as normal as Mrs. Fields talking to her or anyone else. It was her imaginary friend who had always been there when she had needed him.

"I don't know ..."

"*Don't I always tell you where to hide? Haven't I always protected you?*"

"Yes ... but I'm scared of Kate and Owen."

"*I know you are. I'll be there with you.*"

Alanna used her foot to make the swing start rocking. "Yeah ... but you're not real. It's not like you're a prince or anything and you're going to come and save me."

"*I've told you before; you have to come and find me.*"

"That's hard to do when you won't tell me where you are."

"*I can't.*"

"Why?"

"*You have to find me.*"

Alanna gave a tired sigh. "Are you very far away?" she asked, even though she already knew the answer. This was the same conversation she'd had with her invisible friend many times before. "I'll never be able to find you. You're invisible."

"*You will.*" The wind promised. "*You will find me when the time is right. All princesses have to wait for their princes.*"

"Are you a prince?"

"*No, but I know who your prince is, and he's waiting for you, too.*"

"He is? What's he waiting for?" Alanna hurriedly asked, hearing Mrs. Fields and her caseworker opening the back door.

"What do you want me to tell her?"

Matthew stared at Silas as his brother talked to the girl who was destined for him, trying to come up with an answer that wouldn't change the path set ahead for them.

"For you to call out my name."

"*How am I supposed to know his name?*" Silas repeated what the young girl had said.

"You will know without me ever having to tell you."

"*What am I supposed to do until then?*"

Matthew stared at Silas in agony, not wanting to give the answer he had no choice to give.

His brother stared back at him in understanding, well aware of the turmoil he was going through.

"We wait."

Chapter One

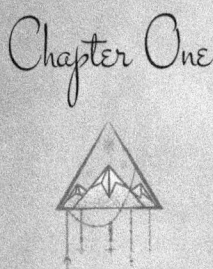

Alanna was jerked awake by the light being turned on in the corridor outside of her jail cell. Groggily raising herself up onto an elbow, she looked to see why the lights had been turned on in the middle of the night. If the deputy who was usually on duty had come to annoy her in the middle of the night, she was going to file a formal complaint for cruel and unusual punishment.

Blinking to clear the sleep out of her eyes, she saw two deputies maneuvering a large man inside the opposite cell. At least, she thought the person was a male. From her viewpoint, she couldn't really tell. All she could discern was, whoever it was, they were large enough that the deputies were having trouble carrying him, and a hoodie hid the back of his head from her.

Tossing the person onto the bunk, the deputies exited the cell, slamming the door closed behind them.

Seeing she was observing them, the deputy who was too young to have such shockingly white hair spoke to the other deputy, whom she had only seen a few times before. "You go on, Larry. I'll be there in a minute."

Walking closer to her cell door, Deputy Porter gave a backward nod of his head. "He won't be bothering you none. Had too good of a time at the fair tonight. You need anything before I turn the lights off?"

"No, I don't need anything, but I'd feel more comfortable if you put him in the other cell and leave the lights on."

"I'm not chancing putting more of a strain on my back than I already have. He weighs a ton. The lights are bright enough to keep you awake and won't do his head any good if he wakes up. If I were you, I'd prefer him sleeping. Only person on duty tonight is the dispatcher. The rest of us are out and about on patrol, or stationed at the fairgrounds."

Alanna swung her legs off the side of the cot. "I don't exactly feel comfortable knowing that I'm sleeping within six feet of someone who has done something illegal to get arrested."

The deputy rattled her cell door. "Hear that?"

"Yes," she gritted out between clenched teeth.

Taking a step back, he rattled the other cell door. "Here that?"

"Yes," she muttered angrily.

"Then you're all good?"

"I guess so," she forced out. At this point, she just wanted him to leave.

The deputy walked back to her door. "Reckon I'll see you in the morning. Want anything in particular for breakfast?"

"Pancakes with a nail file inside would be appreciated."

The deputy shook his head, as if he was taking her sarcastic joke serious. "Sorry, my misses would have my ass if I lost my job when we just found out we're expecting."

"Then no, I don't want anything."

"Suit yourself." He shrugged.

Alanna lay back down as the deputy moved away from the

cell. At least he did make one concession by not turning the light off in the corridor.

Turning to her side to stare toward the other cell now that the deputy had moved out the way, she could see the man's tall form lying on the bunk, on his side, with his back turned toward her. The cell had sat empty since her arrest. Owen had been placed in another cell further down the corridor.

There was no way she was going to be able to go back to sleep, regardless of there being two metal doors separating the cells. She had never been able to sleep with someone else in the room after she had been taken in by the Fields. Owen and Kate had made nights a torture to endure.

The shadowy interior of the cells escalated her fears that came out to play in the dark. Sitting back up, she scrunched herself into a ball, in the corner of her bunk, to stare unblinking at the figure on the other bunk. Hitching her head upward when she nearly nodded off numerous times, she almost screamed out loud when she saw the man suddenly roll over to his back then sit on the side of the bed to look toward her cell.

Other than pressing her back against the wall behind her, Alanna froze. Could he see her? Shards of fear fissured through her body.

Don't panic. Clenching her hands under the blanket until her nails bit into the palms, Alanna talked herself down from her fears so she could think with a clear head and not let the fear overtake her. *He's just sitting there.*

Her clear-headedness was shaken when the figure rose from the bed to stand at the bars of his cell.

"Don't be afraid, Alanna. I'm not going to hurt you."

Alanna put her hand over her mouth to keep from speaking, alarm bells ringing in her mind from hearing him call her by name, knowing she was frightened.

"I feel your fear."

A low husky laugh started to rattle her already shaky resolve to remain calm.

He hung his hands out of the bars casually, as if to show he was weaponless and caged like her, but it didn't lessen the panic which kept her silent.

The laughter stopped, and then she heard a loud, drawn-out sigh.

"You should had grown out of hiding when you're scared."

Pressing her lips together to prevent herself from asking how he knew about her habit, she wished he would move a little to the left so the light would expose the features the loose material of his hood concealed.

"This jail isn't the safe haven you think it is," he warned chillingly. "At what point are you going to be brave enough to quit running and hiding?"

Never, when she knew who was waiting for her outside!

The silent scream echoed throughout the chambers of her mind.

"You've let fear make you a prisoner long before coming here."

"Shut up!" she yelled then slapped a hand over her mouth.

"What's the matter? Did I strike a nerve?"

Alanna dropped her hand. "Did Owen pay you to get arrested to warn me to keep my mouth shut?"

"No one paid me to get arrested, but *I am* here to give a warning. You're not safe here. I'm disappointed that you haven't been able to come up with a better plan, other than to sacrifice your freedom because you're afraid to confront your fears. I expected more from you."

The censure in his voice had her pride taking a nosedive.

"Sorry to disappoint you, but I'm just trying to stay alive the best way I know how."

"Then, if I were you—" The hands hanging out of the jail

cell slid back inside. Her fear skyrocketed when she saw a spark of fire then heard the cell door click open. Her vocal cords froze when he stepped into the corridor to stand outside her door. "—I would take the help being offered to you before it's too late."

Alanna sucked in a deep breath when she was finally able to see the face of the man speaking to her.

Rugged features enforced the impression of strength. An implacable expression showed this man had a self-confidence that only came with hard-earned experience. She wouldn't be such a wimp if she had been built like a linebacker, either. Her whole life would have been different if she had been a man.

"You have a good lawyer—use her. At least give her a fighting chance to help."

"Go back to your cell before I scream," she warned huskily, proud of herself that she was actually able to get the words out.

Sensual lips curled into a mocking smile. "What will you do if I don't? Come on; show me," he urged her softly.

Fear, as always, held her in place.

"You don't have a problem taking risks when it concerns someone else. You're important, too."

She shook her head in denial, even though she knew he couldn't see the motion. She could drop off the face of the earth and no one would notice. Being jailed for the last two months had proven that fact without a doubt.

"I'm waiting."

Her heart stopped at his words. Then Alanna realized he meant he was waiting to see if she would scream, not waiting like the wind had once told her her prince would be. *It's your imagination*, she told herself. Just because his voice curled around her like a warm embrace and his eyes made heat pool in the pit of her stomach didn't mean he was the man she had lost all hope of ever meeting.

She would ask to speak to her attorney tomorrow, if nothing else other than to get a refill on her medication.

"You have become afraid of your own shadow, Alanna. The thing is, all you have to do to be free of your fears is to step out into the light. You believe this jail cell is a form of protection, while in reality, the shadows are consuming you," he warned.

Allana could see the knuckles of his hands gripping the bars turn white.

"Either get this shit straightened out, or I will. I'm not supposed to interfere, but I will." His face became menacing. "My willpower is reaching a breaking point. I'm not a saint."

As he dropped his hands from the bars, Alanna tensed, waiting to see if he was going to open her cell door like he had his.

"Don't ..." she whimpered fearfully, childhood memories flashing back.

Taking a step away from the cell, he gave her the space she needed.

"I will leave without you tonight, but if I have to come back, Alanna, no army will be able to hold me back." Turning, he left down the corridor until he was out of sight. When she heard the main door open and close, she knew he was gone.

Cautiously getting out of bed, she went to the cell bars to glance out the corridor. It was empty.

Catching a slight odor, Alanna sniffed the air. She smelled a woodsy scent combined with smoke. It was the same odor she had caught when the man had opened his cell.

Glancing at the empty cell across from her, she half-convinced herself that the whole thing had been a waking nightmare. Her other realistic half wasn't as gullible, remaining alert for the rest of the night until she finally heard the day shift employees' voices filtering through the old-fashioned airduct. Relieved by the reassuring sounds within shouting distance, she fell into a fitful sleep in which she had the same recurring dream that she'd had since being arrested.

She was locked in a tiny cage.

"Help me!" she screamed in her nightmare. "Help me!"

"I'm coming!" a faint voice would answer.

Each night, the voice had seemed to be drawing closer. Tonight, when he answered, she managed to squeeze her hand and arm through the bars.

"Where are you?" she cried out.

"I'm here."

"Let me out!" Pressing herself against the cage, she tried to reach out farther. "Let me out!" she begged.

"I can't," the husky voice demanded. "You have to come to me, Alanna."

"I'm trapped! I can't!"

"Come to me ..." The voice started to retreat back into the distance. "Come to me ... You're so close ... so close ..."

Chapter Two

God help her, but she was going to kill him. Slowly, to draw out the pleasure.

No, she took that back. She would make it quick. Quick was good. She didn't want to take the chance he would talk her out of strangling him.

Alanna eyed the deputy cleaning the cell across from her while devising several different methods to off him.

"I told the misses I want Rosie's ass in bed at 8:30, no exceptions, and wanting to eat a bowl of cereal at ten isn't one."

Clutching the book she was pretending to read rather than being drawn into an argument that she already knew she didn't stand a chance of winning against the exasperating deputy, Alanna tried to drown out his voice by imagining her hands wrapped around his throat.

Don't break, she told herself, resolved to give him the silent treatment after Deputy Porter had denied he and another deputy had locked someone in the vacant cell last night. She knew good and well she hadn't imagined the hooded prisoner.

"What you want for lunch today?"

It took the deputy repeating the question two times before she realized he had come to stand in front of her cell.

Her resolve broke, worn down by his incessant talking. He never stopped—*ever*—unless the sheriff came looking for him, or Deputy Porter finally became bored enough to seek out helpless victims to impart his brand of wisdom to.

"Doesn't matter. You choose." *You will, anyway*, she thought snidely.

"How about the diner? King shorted us a baked potato yesterday. It'll show him that he'll lose the jail's business if he doesn't keep the quality we expect from him."

"Whatever."

"You're in a pissy mood today, ain't you?"

The sarcastic jab had her doing what she had sworn not to do.

"Why wouldn't I be? You just cleaned a cell, despite pretending no one was in there last night."

The deputy puffed his chest out, as if offended. "You callin' me a liar?"

"I'm saying someone was there. I saw you and another deputy put him on the bed. You even talked to me before you left."

"If that were true, then why wasn't anyone in there this morning when John came in?"

"He left."

The deputy furrowed his brow. "Who did?"

"Whoever was in the cell."

"How he get out? What was his name?"

"You didn't introduce him to me," she snapped. "He unlocked his cell door and walked out."

He wiggled his eyebrows at her. "How he unlock the cell door?"

"I don't know; he just did."

"Sounds like you had a nightmare. I had one the other night. I dreamt—"

"Never mind. It was a nightmare."

She would rather bang her head against the cement blocks than listen to his nightmare. The deputy was wasting his time being a small-town deputy. He could give lessons on torture to international organizations.

"Since you're done cleaning, you can leave."

"Don't take it out on me that your ass is locked up in there. I'm the one the sheriff pulls from patrolling whenever someone gets their ass locked up." Crossing his arms over his chest, the deputy leaned against the bars of her cell. "Personally, I'd rather be driving around in my squad car than being stuck inside, babysitting you. Makes no sense to me why you're even still here instead of that bitch niece of yours."

Alanna angrily tossed the book aside. "Don't call Elizabeth a bitch. Who should still be sitting in jail is Owen, and you released him!"

The deputy lifted a condescending brow at her. "I agree with you, but what I want doesn't count in the eyes of the law about Owen. On the other hand, I think it's hilarious you're still taking up for Elizabeth when she's the one responsible for you looking at some serious time."

"Elizabeth isn't responsible for me getting arrested," she scoffed, trying to resist saying anything else to him, then failing at the pitying way he looked at her. "Mind your own business, and I'll mind mine."

"Treepoint is a small town; everybody knows your business, whether you want them to or not." He shrugged. "Damn if I would put my freedom on the line for anyone, family or not." He gave a disgusted snort. "How much longer you going to sit here, twiddling your thumbs, expecting her to come and save the fucking day? Elizabeth is going to steamroll you into a prison sentence, and you're gonna let her. Then, when you come to your senses at the state pen, you can say Greer told you so," he mocked. "I wish I had a nickel for how many dumbasses have found themselves locked up protecting someone else."

"I haven't done anything wrong, and Elizabeth will testify to that."

"What she waiting for? Why wait until you go to trial?"

"There are mitigating factors you're unaware of."

"*Mitigating factors?* Jeez, you know what that sounds like? A fancy way of saying you're fucked. Have you told your lawyer about this information? The sheriff?" The deputy gave her a pitying look. "Just don't expect her to come visiting you in the state pen when they give you life."

A crunching fear had her jumping up from the bunk to confront him. "You're overexaggerating to get me to talk, and it won't work. *Life*?" she scoffed. "I didn't kill anyone."

The deputy raised his hand, lifting one finger at a time. "Kidnapping, bribery, assault—"

"I did not kidn—" Snapping her jaw closed, Alanna hugged her waist as she turned to give the deputy her back, hiding her expression. "Go away."

"Owen Hudson is telling the sheriff it was all your plan to get Arin not to give the patent away for the vaccine. That you were planning to sell it to the highest bidder."

She pressed her lips together to keep herself from talking.

"He's gonna walk with a sweet deal while your ass rots away."

Her resolve lasted one hot minute before doubt creeped in, undermining her determination.

"My lawyer won't let that happen."

"Diamond is good, but she ain't that good. What you need is a fucking miracle," he ridiculed her.

Unable to take it any longer, Allana spun to face him. "Unless you have one handy, please leave me alone," she pleaded, unable to keep the fear at bay any longer. Why had she allowed herself to get drawn into talking to him? She needed her medication. It put her in a funky headspace where she didn't want to talk.

His discerning gaze bore directly into hers. "I wouldn't say handy"—straightening from the bars, he pulled his pants up his skinny frame—"but I been known to make them happen when someone needs one."

"Is this where you tell me you'll help me out if I do a little something for you?" Giving him a disgusted glance, she sat back down on the bunk.

"You think I'm wanting something sexual from you?"

She disdainfully gave him a withering look. "Aren't you?"

The deputy laughed at her. "Sorry, but my sexual favors are spoken for. I'm a married man. I'm lucky to keep the misses satisfied, much less giving it away to anyone else."

Surprised, she stared at the man who had been a pain in her neck since she had found herself in Treepoint. Men typically didn't reveal they had trouble keeping their partners satisfied.

"Then, what do you want for this *miracle*?"

"There's no price tag attached." He shrugged. "I don't want to be accused of bribery. I have a reputation to maintain in this town. Of course, I don't even know if I can help you with this miracle, *free of charge*, unless you start opening that yapper of yours and tell me why that kin of yours has it out for you."

He wanted her to trust him when she hadn't even trusted her lawyer with the information?

Alanna couldn't believe she was even considering talking to him. She needed her medication. If imagining a prisoner who didn't exist last night hadn't proven that, considering confiding in a man she frankly couldn't stand did.

"Why should I?" Rebuffing him with a careless shrug, she

plopped back down on the bed to reach for the discarded book.

"Woman, Imma just gonna be plain blunt. The only reason I'm even considering helping you is because I know how it is to want to help a family member out. You're between a rock and a hard place. It's no never mind to me what you do. The only reason I'm even thinking about helping you out is from the kindness of my soul."

Was this the same man who, yesterday, had confiscated the baked potato that had come with her dinner when his had been shorted?

Alanna lifted her eyes from the book. "Deputy Porter, if you want to do something from the kindness of your soul, convince my niece to accept my calls."

Alanna knew from the gloating look he gave her that he was going to take pleasure in what he was about to tell her.

"I can't be doing that. Elizabeth doesn't want to talk to you. The sheriff received the paperwork this morning. Elizabeth is seeking a restraining order, preventing you from trying to contact her or be within a hundred feet of her. Said you're threatening her."

Alanna stared at him in shock, fighting back the escalating alarm she had been dealing with since discovering what her niece had become involved in and with whom. Elizabeth had sworn to her that she hadn't had contact with her mother since she graduated from high school.

Reading her expression, the deputy gave her a smart-aleck snort. "What do you think I've been trying to tell you? Your niece is looking out for numero uno. How do you think I know that? Because I'm all about looking out for my own interests. Difference between her and me, though, is I wouldn't throw my own kin under the bus. You need to wise up before she mows your ass down."

"You don't understand. Elizabeth is like my own daughter," Alanna told him numbly.

"Then you raised her for shit. That's why my kids mind me, or else," he huffed out arrogantly.

Alanna felt sorry for any child who had him for a father.

"Your sister know her daughter is a lying bitch?"

Alanna winced at the derogatory way the deputy had referred to her niece.

"Elizabeth is a wonderful person. She's just ..." Alanna pressed her lips together, changing what she had been about to say. "I was trying to help her when that trucker kidnapped me and brought me to Treepoint."

"Really?" He rolled his eyes at her. "That isn't the same story she's been telling everyone else. Of course, her being taped up like a mummy when that trucker found her in the trunk of the car you were sitting in has everyone giving her the benefit of the doubt as to who should be believed. Especially when you're refusing to explain to your lawyer or the sheriff as to why they should believe you over her."

"This is just a misunderstanding." Closing the book, she rose from the bed to walk to where he was standing.

"Which you made no effort to clear yourself of. Why haven't you even asked Diamond to get you out on bail? Damn, I wouldn't be standing here if I wasn't paid to be."

"I have nowhere to go. If I get released, Diamond told me they would monitor me. I don't have the money to stay at the hotel until my case is heard."

"You broke?"

"No, but close." *Not yet*, she conceded silently to herself. "I've already had to use my savings to pay my legal expenses. There isn't much left."

"Sounds like you need a place to stay and a job."

"I don't have a real estate license in Kentucky, and the company I work for is trying to have my license revoked. I asked Diamond about finding a job in town, and she said there aren't any."

"There aren't in town." He nodded.

The deputy confirming her lawyer's assessment of the job market in Treepoint had her feeling defeated. She was at a loss at what to do, feeling as if her life had become quicksand and she was sinking fast.

"*But* I might know of one in the city limits."

She gripped a cell bar. "What is it? I'll take anything."

"It ain't no hoity-toity job like being a real estate agent," he warned.

"I don't care as long it pays me so I can afford a hotel room."

"The job comes with bed and board."

She gripped the jail cell bar harder until her nails bit into palm of her hand. The extra money she saved could increase the money for the rising legal fees. She also wouldn't be a sitting duck if the man from last night did exist and come back as he'd warned.

"Had lunch over at the diner yesterday, overheard the Colemans are looking for a housecleaner to clean some of the boys' homes on their property. Might need to do a spot of cooking for them, too. Just telling you what I overheard." He shrugged. "You'll have to get Diamond to check it out for you."

"I'm a good cleaner, and I love cooking." She didn't, but if he could lie about last night, she could lie about that. "I make a great—"

The deputy raised his hand to stop her from continuing. "It ain't me you'll have to convince. Diamond gonna have to convince the judge to let you out on bail, then convince Silas Coleman to hire you, so I wouldn't get my hopes up until you talk to her."

"Do you mind calling her and asking her to come see me?"

"Can do." The deputy turned to leave.

"Thank you. I really appreciate your help. If this works out, I'll owe you big time," she said sincerely. Then she hastened to clarify what she meant, not wanting him to get any wrong ideas. "As long as it doesn't involve sex."

"Woman, you're the one with sex on the brain, not me. Jesus, what's with women nowadays? I remember the good ole days when women were too embarrassed to talk about it. So, you know, around these parts, the word *sex* is considered a four-letter word coming from a woman with a man in the room."

"Then, how does you helping me benefit you?" she asked skeptically.

"Puts my ass back in my cruiser, where it belongs."

Alanna watched the deputy swagger off as if he owned the world as butterflies filled her stomach. He seemed just a little too cheerful when all he was going to get out of helping her was a return to his normal duties.

The first bloom of happiness at possibly getting of jail faded into apprehension. Why did she feel as if she had just unwittingly sold her soul after bargaining with a fast-talking devil in Kentucky?

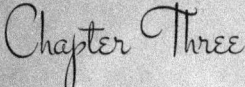

Chapter Three

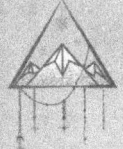

"Mrs. Bates, were you able to contact Mr. Coleman about the housekeeping job Deputy Porter told me about?"

Being in the lawyer's presence never failed to make her feel as if she had royally screwed her life up. Immaculately dressed, from the stylish hair to the tips of her shoes, the lawyer didn't have a hair or thread out of place. Mrs. Bates appeared to have every aspect of her life within her control, while she couldn't even control what she could pick to eat without the deputy switching the order to what *he* wanted.

Glancing up from her briefcase after taking out a legal pad and ink pen, Mrs. Bates's rigid expression showed she was expecting the same lack of cooperation from her that she had received when they had talked previously. "I did. Silas said he would stop by to interview you when he comes to town this morning."

"It didn't put him off that I'm in jail?"

"No. He was more concerned about when you could start."

Her lawyer seemed to be just as surprised at the lack of concern as she was.

"Did he ask what charges had been pressed against me?" she probed, embarrassed about having to meet a potential employer in jail.

"No, I don't imagine Silas needed to. Everyone in town knows why you were arrested."

Cringing inwardly about what must be being said about her, Alanna began wondering what kind of man would be willing to hire someone in jail for kidnapping and attempted extortion.

Withering shame had her seeking to reclaim what little pride she could in front of the other woman.

"I hope he doesn't think I'll let him take advantage of the situation and expect more than cleaning and cooking."

"I didn't come out and ask if sex was in the job description when I spoke to him over the phone. I thought I would save that question for when he comes to interview you for the job."

Alanna tried not to blush under her lawyer's gaze. Self-conscious, she tugged the orange sleeve of the scrub top she was wearing over her wrist. God, she missed wearing regular clothes. The ugly bright orange scrubs she had been forced to wear since her arrest never let her forget for a second she was a prisoner. Compared to the other woman, she felt like a carrot stick. Orange was definitely not her color. She resembled a pumpkin.

She envied the clothes her lawyer was wearing, from the Louis Vuitton heels to the light gray skirt with a matching blazer, which was set off by a Milano purple silk blouse tucked neatly inside the waistband. If she didn't feel at a disadvantage already at her lawyer's polished appearance compared to the jailhouse thin scrubs she was wearing, the cool air blowing directly down on her side of the table just put the cherry on top of the downward spiral her life had taken.

"I've arranged for the interview. Now, are you finally willing—"

"Do you mind switching places with me?" Alanna cut her off. "I'm freezing under this vent," she explained when the other woman stared at her coolly.

"Certainly."

They switched places, and Alanna folded her arms across her chest defensively. "They keep this place like an igloo. What's the temperature outside?" she asked before the lawyer could resume talking, not above taking advantage of any distraction to put off having to discuss her case. "It's fall. You would think the sheriff would have switched over to heat instead of keeping the air conditioning on high."

Alanna saw the woman glance upward toward the vent with a baffled expression before returning her gaze to her. "It is a little warm out today, but I'll speak to the sheriff before I leave."

Was the irritation she heard in her voice because she thought she would leave empty-handed yet again? Alanna couldn't blame her. She had left the lawyer to defend her without giving her a leg to stand on.

Clasping her cold hands together on the table, she tried to gauge how much she should disclose to a woman who looked as if the scariest thing she had ever had to deal with was stepping on a piece of gum in her designer shoes.

"Why did you choose to represent me instead of Elizabeth?" Alanna asked curiously.

The lawyer closed her briefcase and scooted her chair closer to the table. "Because, when I met you, you reminded me a little of myself. I'm good at hiding my emotions as well."

Alanna raised a hand to press her fingers against her temple, the slight headache she had woken up to that morning becoming more pronounced.

"Deputy Porter told me you're married to the sheriff?"

"I am." The lawyer answered after giving her a questioning glance.

"Happily?"

"How does how happy my marriage is pertain to me defending you in a court of law?"

Alanna dropped her hand back to the table to lean her face closer to Mrs. Bates, wanting to see if her eyes would reveal the truth for the question she was about to ask. "Because I want to know if he's going to protect you with every beat of his heart, or if you'll be on your own."

The woman met her eyes without shying away, nor did she lean away from their faces being just an inch apart. "We're very happily married. You're worried about my protection? Is that why you've refused to answer any of my questions?"

"Partially."

Her gaze became discerning. "You've been protecting Elizabeth, too."

"You have no concept of how dangerous Owen is." Alanna settled back in her chair. "Mrs. Bates, refer me to another attorney to defend me. Preferably a man."

The lawyer's shoulders arched back, as if she had just been insulted. "You don't think I can defend you equally as well as a man?"

Alanna shook her head. "That isn't what I'm saying. Owen is dangerous. He won't like that you will be defending me, and the fact that you're a woman will only make him happier if he decides to go after you."

Her lawyer gave her a steely-eyed stare. "If he comes after me, he'll end up with more than he bargained for."

She may think that now, but Alanna had no doubt that the lawyer was going to rue the day she didn't take her up on the offer to get someone else to take over defending her.

"I think you're going to end up with more than you bargained for ..." Alanna couldn't consciously let the woman walk blindly into her nightmare life without letting her know what she was getting into. "Owen is sick. He gets his kicks by hurting women ... Mrs. Bates, you have no clue ..." Alanna chewed on her bottom lip.

"I have repeatedly asked you to call me Diamond."

Alanna refused to use Diamond's first name in person. She had to remain detached from her.

Her lawyer gave her a quizzical smile. "I'm well aware of Owen Hudson's attitude where women are concerned. I'm curious as to why you're more concerned for my safety versus your own?"

Alanna stood up, unable to sit still another moment. Being couped up in the small rooms was getting to her.

"Oh, I'm terrified of him." Alanna nodded her head as she spoke. "Why do you think I haven't been anxious to get out? At least, in jail, I don't have to be afraid when I close my eyes."

"Then what made you decide to finally talk to me?"

"Because I would rather take my chances with Owen than having to deal with Deputy Porter monitoring me morning, noon, and night. Is he normally so irritating, or has he been doing it just to get me to talk to you?"

Mrs. Bates's lips twitched in humor. "Sadly, abrasiveness comes to Greer naturally. He takes a lot of patience to deal with."

Alanna thought that was the understatement of the century.

"Deputy Porter would make a saint want to strangle him."

"As much as we could discuss how obnoxious Greer is until we're old and gray, I would really like to hear how you found yourself in this situation."

"You don't believe I'm the mastermind of kidnapping my niece?"

The lawyer narrowed her eyes on her. "I need you to be one hundred percent honest with me. Any discussions between us are protected under attorney-client privilege. I won't even disclose anything to my husband without your permission. So, let's begin again, this time with you being completely truthful. Elizabeth has no family connection to you. She's not your niece. You have no immediate siblings, nor any half- or stepsiblings."

"You've done your homework." Alanna stopped chewing on her lip when she tasted a tinge of blood.

"I have. Listen, there's nothing more I can do without your help. I can't defend someone who doesn't want to be defended. Tell Greer I said hi ..." Her lawyer started to rise from the table.

Alanna sighed, sitting back down. "I entered the foster care system when I was four. My parents went out for a hike and never came back. I still remember I was watching cartoons when the woman who was babysitting me freaked out when they were late picking me up. Instead of my parents coming back, a police officer and a woman from Social Services came to tell me that they wouldn't be back. They had fallen off a path, which had been declared unsafe. I don't know how familiar you are with group homes, but believe me, especially in a large city, it was a hell of an adjustment."

"I can imagine."

Alanna grimaced. "I don't think you can. It was horrible. The older children picked on the younger ones. Foster homes were few and far between, and they usually picked the cute ones, or the children who could contribute to chores, who don't require as much supervision. I was sent to two foster homes, and they didn't last because, both times, my foster family found themselves expecting." Alanna folded her hands over each other to hide their trembling. "I met Kate when I was six."

"Kate?"

Mrs. Bates picked up her ink pen and started writing on

the legal pad.

"Elizabeth's mother."

"What's her full name?"

"Kate Easton."

"That's not the name I found listed as the name for Elizabeth's mother."

"Kate adopted Elizabeth."

"Legally?"

"I believe so." Alanna shrugged. "But, with Kate, anything is possible."

"You met Ms. Easton when you were in foster care?"

"She was older than me"—Alanna nodded—"and had been in and out foster homes since she was a baby. She took me under her wing, kept the older children from hurting me, but more than that, she called me her little sister. I didn't feel so alone anymore. I felt loved for the first time since my parents had died.

"When a foster family was found for her, it devastated me. I cried for several days. It was like losing my parents all over again. I felt as if the rug had been pulled out from under me again. About a month later, when Kate came back from lunch, she was there. She told me they had sent her back because of her behavior. She told me she had deliberately misbehaved just so she would be sent back. She told me she had missed her little sister. I fell for her lies hook, line, and sinker." Alanna shook her head at herself in self-disgust.

"At first, I was happy Kate had been sent back, but little by little, even at that young age, I started noticing something was off about her. She would lie to the staff constantly when she got in trouble by blaming other children. The more Kate disliked you, or even worse, didn't give in to her demands, the more trouble they got into. The staff liked her and believed the lies she would tell them. If I said anything to her about the lies she told, when I left the room, I would come back and find some of my things had disappeared or been destroyed. The older we grew, the more afraid of her I became.

"I was given to another foster family, and I was thrilled to be away from her. When I was sent back, I prayed she wouldn't be there. She was. There was no place where I could hide that she couldn't find me. She would watch me like a hawk, and the more frightened I became of her, the more she liked it. When she discovered something scared me, she would hone in on it, and if I didn't do something she wanted, Kate would punish me by using those fears against me. The harshness of the punishment depended on how angry she was at me." Alanna didn't go into any of the details of the methods Kate had used against her.

Taking a jerky breath, she continued on under her lawyer's scrutiny. "It came to the point I was afraid to be alone with her and would give my things away rather than see them end up with her or be destroyed."

Her lips turned upward in a pained smile. "Finally, I was given a reprieve when Kate was sent to a new foster home. I remember sleeping for two days straight with her gone. I wasn't the only one glad to see her away. Out of thirty kids, she had everyone terrified of her. Truthfully, I think some of the staff were, too, by that point.

"About six months after Kate left, I was taken to a new foster home. They didn't tell me it was the same one where Kate was living. The only good part of that foster home was the Fields family. They were wonderful to me. They were to all the children. Despite having a child of their own, they had taken in a boy the same age as Kate, then me. However, there wasn't a day that went by that Kate wouldn't throw in my face that I was only there because she had told Mrs. Fields she missed her little sister."

"She wanted you indebted to her," Mrs. Bates surmised.

"Exactly." Alanna nodded. "Of course, I was too young to

realize it at the time. I was too afraid of losing the Fields. They were really good people. I had grown close to their son, Sam, who was younger than me.

"Kate started using my affection for Sam against me. She would threaten to do something and blame it on me so I would be sent back to the group home. Needless to say, I walked on eggshells around her," she said wryly.

Her lawyer gave her a commiserating glance. "She was a Regina George."

"Kate could run circles around Regina."

"You mentioned another foster child was there …"

Alanna gave her a curt nod. "Yes, there was—Owen Hudson. "

The two women made eye contact.

"And despite what your husband, the sheriff, may have told you about Owen's past history, I can say, with absolute certainty, not all of the crimes he committed have been documented. In case you're under any delusion about what Owen is capable of, it doesn't even begin to scratch the surface of the ugliness inside of him. The more you unearth, the uglier it will get."

"I'm not afraid of him." Mrs. Bates gave her an unwavering stare.

Alanna gave the elegant lawyer a pitying glance. "You're not understanding what I'm trying to tell you." Placing her hands down flat on the table, Alanna leaned forward. "I've been trying to warn you that Owen isn't the only one to be afraid of. Imagine someone getting joy from hurting the most innocent of creatures, then imagine that same person being a pawn of a woman who gets the same sick kicks, and you still wouldn't be able to comprehend what those two are capable of when they don't get their way. Sadly, if you continue to represent me and get on their radar, you're going to be finding that out for yourself.

"Kate will find every miniscule detail about your life. There will be no part of your life untouched until she discovers what will hurt you the most. And then ... God help you when she does. That's when she'll get Owen to hurt or destroy what you value the most, or even worse, she does it herself. Mrs. Bates, do you and your family a favor—take that expensive briefcase and run as far as you can from my case," Alanna begged her.

Instead of being frightened, her lawyer gave her a mocking smile.

Alanna wanted to shake the woman for disregarding her warning so lightly until she noticed the steely determination in her eyes.

"I'm not running. If either Kate Easton or Owen Hudson come after me, they'll get more than they bargained for."

Alanna's shoulders slumped. By the time Owen and Kate were done with Mrs. Bates, the lawyer would be lucky to have a nail to hang her fancy law degree on.

"Is this the reason you've been refusing to speak to me and the sheriff? Because they've been using something you care about against you?"

Alanna nodded, defeated. She had to get out of jail. She couldn't take another day of Deputy Porter. She had never committed a crime in her life, but if she heard his irritating voice one more time, a capital murder charge was in her near future.

"You're afraid they'll hurt Elizabeth," Mrs. Bates guessed. "She isn't talking, either. Is that because it was her idea to hold up the patent or—"

"She was protecting me," Alanna cut her off.

Her lawyer arched a brow at her. "She protected you by getting you arrested for her kidnapping?"

"I may be sitting in jail, but at least I'm still alive."

Chapter Four

"How long have you two been protecting each other?" Her lawyer asked without looking up from the pad she was writing on.

"I've been trying to protect Elizabeth since Kate showed up with her when I was a senior in high school. She was waiting beside my car, with Elizabeth, and told me she was her daughter. I knew she wasn't Kate's biological daughter because of her age.

"Kate asked me to watch her while she went to a doctor appointment. After that, Kate would randomly show up, expecting me to watch Elizabeth whenever she needed a sitter. I'd usually take her to a restaurant or a movie."

"Why didn't you just tell her no?"

"Because I couldn't imagine Kate being a mother. I wanted to find out from Elizabeth how she was with Kate. I didn't want to accuse Kate of being guilty of mistreating Elizabeth if she was innocent. It had been a few years since I had seen Kate. She could have changed. Being responsible for a child could have softened her. I watched for every sign." Even now, she second-guessed the decision not to have just disappeared with Elizabeth.

"You wanted to intervene, to get her away from Ms. Easton." Mrs. Bates sympathetic gaze wasn't the judgmental one she had expected.

"Oh yes, but Elizabeth would never tell me anything I could use so I could go to the authorities. She would only say how happy she was, that she loved Kate.

"When I graduated from college and was able to find a job and move into an apartment, Kate would bring Elizabeth more often, and we grew even closer. She would spend two or three days at a time with me before Kate would come back. I would constantly ask Elizabeth if she had met Owen or if Kate would bring a man around her who looked like him, and she would tell me no. She was lying to me. I could see it in her eyes.

"I took another job and used the money to hire a private investigator so I could go to the police. Three days after I hired the investigator, he disappeared. I went to the police when I found out. I told them that I believed Kate and Owen were responsible. I begged the detective not to mention me and to look into Kate's relationship with Elizabeth. The detective came to my work a week later to inform me that Owen was living in another state, and Kate hadn't even known she was being investigated, nor had they found any proof that I had even hired the investigator. Kate stopped bringing Elizabeth after."

Her lawyer stopped writing. "What did you do then?"

"I tried to hire another investigator to find Kate and Elizabeth. The next day, my foster mother was found dead at the bottom of her basement steps, and the investigator's daughter died in a car wreck the next day. Before you ask, yes, I went back to the police. Both deaths were ruled to be accidents."

The responsibility she felt for those three deaths would haunt her for the rest of her life.

"But you don't think they were?"

Alanna was at last seeing wariness enter her lawyer's eyes.

Pushing the anguish aside, she answered Mrs. Bates's question, "No, I think Owen was responsible for both. Neither Mrs. Fields's husband, nor Sam, believed her death was an accident, either.

"I moved away when they tried to talk to me. I already had three deaths on my conscience; I wasn't going to get them killed by telling them who I believed was responsible. I was beginning to think Kate was out of my life permanently, that I had moved far enough away it wouldn't be worth her time to contact me again."

"But she did."

Alanna nodded. "Two years later, and she brought Elizabeth with her. This time, I tried to question Elizabeth, but she was even more secretive. I realized, to keep Elizabeth in my life, I was going to have keep my mouth shut and just be there when she asked me for help. The day she turned eighteen was when she asked me to help her get away from Kate. We left that afternoon and moved to another state after she promised me she would have no contact with Kate, and if she found us, she would tell me immediately.

"Elizabeth lived with me until she graduated from college and Arin hired her. She even moved out of our apartment when she found a place with roommates. I was surprised when she moved out. We got along well, and I was busy most of the time with work, but I could understand her wanting to go out on her own."

Mrs. Bates looked up from writing her notes to frown. "You don't think so now?"

"No, I think Kate found her, and she was trying to hide the fact from me. I had already started a new life in Ohio for her, and she didn't want me to have to run again to protect her. The next thing I knew, Arin called to tell me Elizabeth had been kidnapped."

"It would have been much simpler if, when Arin called you, you told her about Kate and Owen."

Running her fingers through her hair, Alanna tried to explain, "I wasn't sure they were the ones responsible. I was unaware Kate had found her."

Closely watching her expression, the lawyer gave her a slight nod, showing she believed her. "How did you end up in the car with Hudson? Were you aware Elizabeth was in the trunk?"

"Two of the owners of empty homes that I sold complained about finding trash and unmade beds when they did their walk-throughs. One of them had cameras and had put up the video for me to watch. I recognized Owen and Elizabeth in them."

"You should have immediately—"

Alanna put up a hand to stop what her lawyer was about to say. "I've told myself that a million times, but I didn't. I was too afraid Owen would kill Elizabeth to prevent himself from getting charged with kidnapping. I went to each of the houses that I hadn't been sold yet. Luckily, I caught sight of Owen pulling out of one of them and followed him. He must have noticed me and pulled over in a parking lot. When I confronted him and told him I wanted to know where Elizabeth was, he told me he would drive me to her. Stupidly, I got in the car, and instead of taking me to her, he wanted to know how I knew he had Elizabeth."

"He wanted to know who else knew," Mrs. Bates murmured under her breath.

"Yes, but I'd already learned that lesson—not to involve anyone else with him and Kate. I was still trying to convince him that I hadn't told anyone when the car door opened, and I was dragged out by the trucker and his legion of friends."

"You had no idea Elizabeth was in the trunk?"

"No, if I had, I would have called the police. He must have put her in the trunk before I arrived at the house."

Her lawyer raised a questioning brow. "What I don't get is: why, when there were so many men around when she was taken out of the trunk, and then again when she was released from the back of the semi, didn't she clear you?"

Alanna's voice became strained with pain. "Because the other person she was afraid of wasn't there."

"Ms. Easton."

"Kate is just as dangerous as Owen. It's been so many years since I've been around her. I don't even know if there are any other stooges she has willing to do her dirty work for her."

"So, Elizabeth thought the safest place for you was in jail."

"If I could talk to her, Mrs. Bates, I'm sure I can convince her to—"

"Please, call me Diamond, at least when we're not in court. Every time you call me Mrs. Bates, I look around for Knox." Her lawyer laid her pencil down and got serious. "You are to make no attempt to talk to Elizabeth. Do you understand?" she said sternly.

"But—"

"I would do what she's advising you. Mrs. Bates is the best lawyer in town."

Alanna jerked in her seat, turning around to see a man standing in the doorway behind her. Taken aback at not hearing the door open, she stared at him blankly before realizing he must be the potential employer Mrs. Bates had contacted for her.

"Alanna"—Mrs. Bates rose from her chair—"this is Silas Coleman."

Silas Coleman stepped forward, taking the hand Mrs.

Bates extended. When their hands dropped back to their sides, he turned toward her, and Alanna extended her hand as well. Finding her hand engulfed in his large one, she nearly jerked it back, feeling a sense of déjà vu.

Had she met him before?

Glancing up from their clasped hands and into his kind eyes, Alanna felt as if she'd been engulfed in a huge blanket of comfort. Her hand began trembling in his as she fought back taking a step forward to lay her head on his chest and burst with the tears that she had been holding back since she found out Elizabeth had been kidnapped.

"It's a pleasure to meet you, Alanna."

"It's nice meeting you, Mr. Coleman," she managed to choke out, overwhelmed by new-found emotions she had never felt before.

Why did she feel as if everything was going to be all right? His reassuring presence made her feel that she was no longer standing on her own against the world.

Silas Coleman was the one who broke the contact, turning back to her lawyer with a serious expression on his face. "Let's get this ball rolling. Mrs. Bates, when can I expect my new housekeeper to start?"

Chapter Five

"Are you sure it isn't too tight? I can turn around and have the sheriff loosen it some more."

Alanna looked up from staring at the ankle monitor strapped to her ankle. "No, the strap feels fine."

Silas Coleman nodded at her without removing his eyes from the road. She had expected to feel uncomfortable being alone with him for the first time. Their meeting two days ago had been brief, mainly with him describing the job duties he expected to be done. None of it seemed to be complicated; mainly some housekeeping for his brothers' different homes located on his family's property.

Alanna unobtrusively gave her employer a side-long glance as he drove, still disconcerted by the emotions that had come over her from the moment she turned around to see him. It was as if all the turmoil, fear, and worry inside of her had melted away, like fog dissipates in the bright light of day.

Silas Coleman's comforting presence had settled her nerves when she was led into the courthouse and saw him sitting in the room where her hearing was going to be held. When the judge had granted her release with the stipulation she couldn't leave Treepoint and had to wear an ankle monitor to ascertain she remained on the boundary of Mr. Coleman's property unless she had a trial date, or scheduled to meet with her lawyer. The sheriff was to be notified before leaving the Colemans' property and receive his permission to do so.

The stipulations didn't bother her. She would have sold her soul to get away from the deputy's constant presence.

"I appreciate you taking a chance on giving me a job, Mr. Coleman," Alanna said, breaking the silence in the truck.

"You might as well call me Silas. Save on the confusion after you meet my brothers. That way, we'll know which one of us you're talking to." Silas Coleman's gaze remained fixed on the curvy road.

Alanna averted her gaze from studying his to stare out of the front windshield. "You said there are eight of you?"

"Yes, plus, my sister, her husband, and son." Silas took his eyes off the road to give her a brief smiling glance. "Have you started regretting your decision to take the job?"

"No, I've never been afraid of hard work. I'm just amazed you're all still living together on the same property. Normally, I would think at least one would have moved away."

They hadn't discussed the ages of his brothers during the short interview. Skittish of saying the wrong thing and have Silas deciding against hiring her, she hadn't asked many questions. She was regretting it now. At least she would have been better prepared for what was waiting for her.

"None of us consider ourselves normal. The boys and I prefer keeping to our mountain. We leave the globe-trotting to our sister, or at least she used to. Ginny's pretty much settled down with her husband in their new home since they had little Freddy. Every now and then, they go on a short trip for Ginny's work. Not so much since she found herself expecting again. That's why I decided to hire someone. Ginny's been doing the job I'm giving you, but the boys and I don't want her to keep overtaxing herself. She'll still help out," he added, giving her a searching look, as if he was scaring her off. "Ginny won't be able to stop herself. I'm just trying to give her a break from the heavier chores she shouldn't be doing anyway."

"That's nice of you." Alanna wondered which heavy chores Silas and his brothers didn't want their sister to do anymore. "Just let me know which chores you don't want her doing, and I'll make sure I take care of them before she can."

"I don't expect you to take over the heavier chores. All I want you to do is text me when you see her lifting over five pounds or climbing anything that is over three inches off the floor."

"I don't have a cell phone," she told him, embarrassed. Not wanting to share the details of how she had lost her phone, Alanna gave him a grateful glance when he just shrugged.

"We have short range radios. I also have a spare cell phone you can use."

With every word he spoke, Alanna liked him more and more. She cautioned herself. Mr. Coleman couldn't be as nice as he seemed, yet something about him was able to bypass the normal wariness which hindered her from making friends.

She slammed an imaginary foot down on mental brakes to put a stop to becoming friendly with him. He was her employer; letting a friendship develop between him or with any of his family could be detrimental to their health.

"Thank you. You can take the price of the phone and the cost of cell service out of my pay."

"That won't be necessary. It's just been sitting in a drawer."

"I insist." Keeping interactions on a business level from the start would save them from possible heartbreak down the road. Kate and Owen would be looking for opportunities to keep her in their control.

As Silas drove, Alanna took the opportunity to stare out at the scenery. Movement from Silas had her turning her head to the side.

"Do you mind not rolling the window down?" she asked, seeing what he was doing.

Rolling the window back up, Silas gave her a surprised look.

"Sorry, allergies," Alanna brusquely explained, averting her gaze back to the side window without further explanation.

"Might need to get some medication for them. I'm afraid you're not going to avoid being outside to get to my brothers' homes."

When she had been told she would be cleaning his brothers' homes, she had nearly refused the job. She hated being outside with a passion.

"It's not a big deal unless the wind is blowing."

"That's unfortunate. I prefer being outside than being inside, but then I don't have any allergies."

"I'll be fine once my medication kicks in," she said absently with her mind on them passing the spot where she had been arrested. The house sitting on a hill above the parking lot was where she had jerked the steering wheel out of the trucker's hand, who had forced her to accompany him to the tiny town she had never heard of before; where she had found herself landed in their jail. It was a stark reminder of how she had failed to find Elizabeth before it escalated to her being accused of the crime that Kate had devised. Alanna was sure Kate was behind the plan to extort Arin, Elizabeth's boss. Owen couldn't tie his own shoes without Kate's help.

Preoccupied by her thoughts, she reached into her jacket pocket to reaffirm the medication Mrs. Bates had filled for her was still safely inside. Once she was back on her medication, the wind talking to her would be muted, and she wouldn't have to be worried she would slip up and talk to someone who wasn't there. She had been on the medication when she confided to Sam that she could talk to the wind, and he talked back. He had told his mother, who had grown concerned enough to take her to a psychiatrist.

Her psychiatrist had prescribed her pills to block out of the voice. She learned quickly that while taking the pills made her feel as if she was living on Mars, it was better than having Mrs. Fields reconsidering being her foster mom. Alanna had seen the worry in her eyes whenever Sam was in the room with her. Terrified of being sent back to the group home, she had taken them.

Once she had moved into her apartment, she had weaned herself off until a coworker overheard her talking to someone without seeing anyone nearby. The wind had stopped talking to her years before, yet she inevitably found herself asking for advice when she was stressed over something even though she knew the wind wouldn't answer. Two valuable lessons had been learned the hard way. People were terrified of anyone being different, especially if involved with someone hearing voices and talking out loud to themselves. They assumed you were a psycho who took orders from your pets. The other lesson was, keeping her medication in her system placed a buffer on the emotional turmoil which made her want to talk to make-believe beings every time she felt a breeze.

Silas' turning into a driveway that couldn't be seen from the road brought a knot to her stomach. In her job as a realtor, she had to appear friendly and outgoing. Inside, she was a bundle of nerves, monitoring their movements and reactions if they came too close to her. During the pandemic, she had been able to keep a space between her and clients without drawing any notice. She would move away if they inadvertently came within a few inches of her.

She wasn't looking forward to meeting such a large group of people. Memories of being overwhelmed when she had been a child and taken to the group home came back to taunt her.

Unexpectantly, the house Silas pulled up to eased the knot in her stomach. She could tell the home was old, but well cared for. Alanna could imagine the two-story house being used in a calendar or book for Southern Living with the surrounding trees giving it a picturesque setting. Visions of a big dinner table, with a mother cooking and children playing happily inside, brought a lump to her throat.

A happy family had been lost to her with her parents' deaths. Instead, she had grown up with children who had been taken out of her life without any notice. Some years, she went to school without knowing who she would be sharing a bedroom with that night, or worse, have an empty bed where before it had been filled with another girl she had slept next to for months.

Because of Kate, she had learned never to get attached to any of her possessions, but being a ward of the state had taught her it was just as risky to develop any affection to anyone she came into contact with. Even with the Fields family, she had never truly given them a place in her heart, too afraid of them being ripped out of her life without any warning.

Indulging herself with make-believe fantasies about what it must have been like to grow up in the large home, she was startled out of her imaginings by the opening of the truck door.

"I think I solved the mystery of why none of your family wants to leave this place," she said, getting out.

Silas tensed as she got out of the truck. Hastily, she moved away, reasoning he shared the same dislike of people being in his personal space.

"Why's that?" he asked, watching her move away.

"This place is beautiful. It looks like a television set in a Hallmark movie."

Silas made a wry face. "Not hardly. It won't take long before that illusion is dispelled. Matthew and Isaac work in a building not far from here. They have been known to swear a blue streak when one of their creations doesn't turn out."

"Creations?"

"They do metal work," he explained. "Stop by anytime. Matthew and Isaac love to show off their skills."

Alanna didn't respond to the invitation. The best part of the job Silas was giving her was the ability to work on her own. It had been her main motive to become a realtor. Other than showing homes, much of the work was done over the phone or in her office at the realty firm. Other than noncommittal greetings and group meetings, the majority of her time had been spent alone.

"Let me show you where you'll be living."

She expected him to continue toward the large house, but he took off to the side. Surprised, she followed him, walking over two small rises.

Where were they going? She had never been good at being out of her comfort zone. Keeping her life on an even kneel had been paramount to her after a childhood filled with upheavals. She had managed to do that until Elizabeth disappeared and she found herself in Treepoint. All she wanted was to get back to the normal life she had made for herself.

"Matthew and Isaac's work building." Silas pointed out as they passed a lone structure set to the side. It was the size of a small house.

The trees surrounding them grew denser. Becoming wary when they started through a corpse of trees, Alanna prepared herself to take off running if Silas made any sudden moves toward her. Her imagination was starting to get the better of her, seeing how secluded the Coleman's property was from town and neighboring homes.

"Almost there. Sorry about the walk, but I thought you would appreciate the privacy ..."

"After being locked up in jail?" she finished for him.

Silas gave her an amused look. "To escape being surrounding by family."

Blushing, Alanna gave him an embarrassed look. "Sorry. I was being oversensitive."

"I would be, too," he excused her, "if I was locked up for something I didn't do."

Alanna looked at him questioningly. "How do you know I'm innocent? You've only talked to me for, like, fifteen minutes total."

"Other than being a great judge of character, I know you're innocent because Diamond Bates wouldn't represent you otherwise."

At his explanation, she felt as if a tiny weight had been taken off her injured pride.

"Thank you," she said. "I appreciate you giving me a chance while I get everything straightened out with the authorities."

"Don't thank me yet."

Ever since she had stepped out of the truck, an eerie feeling had overtaken her, as if something or someone was aware she was there. She glanced toward Silas as he talked; fear assailed her at his serious expression. Tensing, she prepared to run if he so much as ...

"I should have asked you this before you took my job offer," he continued. "There's a part of the job that you might not want to do that only a woman can."

Alanna swallowed the lump of fear in her throat. "What?" she asked, expecting the worst.

"Have you ever milked a goat?"

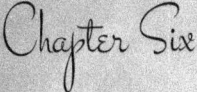

Chapter Six

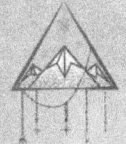

"No." Breaking into relieved laughter, Alanna started walking again. "But I'm game. I like animals."

"Have you ever been around goats before?"

"No. Why?" she asked curiously.

"Never mind, then. They're wonderful creatures."

Alanna was finally catching on that Silas was teasing her, as he had caught on to her nervousness.

"Is there a reason why only a woman can milk the goats?"

"Nope. None at all, other than the goats prefer a woman's touch. Ginny will show you how."

"Okay." She didn't know much about animals and had never been within ten miles of a goat. They looked cute in pictures. She couldn't imagine it being hard to do.

Coming out of the trees, Alanna saw a trailer set in a small clearing.

"It doesn't look like much," Silas went up the three steps to open the metal door.

Haltingly, she went up after him to enter the trailer. She was out in the middle of nowhere, with a man she knew little to nothing about. If not for Greer Porter, she would have asked Silas to drive her back to town. She'd lived in huge cities her whole life. Treepoint presented one culture shock after another.

The small trailer sitting alone, removed from neighbors within shouting distance, had her pulse leaping in fear. She was a city girl at heart, so living here was going to be an adjustment.

Stepping inside the trailer, she was immediately struck by how homey it felt.

"Jody moved in with Jacob so you'd have your own place."

The trailer was farther away from the road, so unless anyone was familiar with the Colemans' property, it would go unseen. The con was it was even more isolated than she had expected.

"Thank you. I don't want any of you to be displaced from your home just to accommodate me. I would be perfectly happy anywhere—"

"Jody doesn't mind. He's usually over at Jacob's, anyway. Let me show you around. It's small, but should have everything you need. If you do need something, just let me know, and I can order it for you. Might take a couple of days, unless you need it quicker, then I can go to town."

"You don't go to town first?"

"Not unless I have to. Most of businesses or people in town aren't very friendly toward us. I'm afraid once people hear that you work for us, the welcome mat won't be coming out."

Alanna was tempted to ask him why, yet didn't want another reason to ask him to drive her back to the cell at the sheriff's office. Besides, probably everyone in town assumed she was guilty of the charges pressed against her anyway, and they had hired her. She wasn't exactly in any position to throw stones at anyone.

The living room had two plush sofas, a wide screen television hanging on the wall, and Alanna noticed an electric fireplace.

"The space is much roomier than I expected from the outside."

"That's why Jody bought it," Silas said, coming to a stop at the kitchenette. "The refrigerator and freezer are full. Ginny checked to make sure you had all the staples. Tomorrow, I'll show you where we keep our supplies. You can take anything you want if you find nothing that appeals to you here."

Moving past the table with four chairs, they went down a small hallway. A pretty vase had been filled with a variety of flowers and sat in the middle of the table.

"The flowers are beautiful." Alanna paused long enough to touch one of the delicate blooms.

"Ginny must have brought them when she was here," he said before moving on. "This is a half-bath." He didn't open the door as he walked forward another couple of steps to another door. Opening it, he entered to turn on the light. "Jody emptied the dresser and closet for you."

"I don't need that much space. I actually don't have any clothes other than what I'm wearing." She might as well be honest about it, she told herself. It's not like Silas and his family members wouldn't begin to notice when she showed up to work each day wearing the same pair of light denim slacks and blue lace sleeveless top.

Silas was unfazed by her admission. "Diamond took care of that for you. She said you didn't have any of your own things, so she picked out a few things to tie you over until you're able to go shopping. Said just to call her when you want to go shopping, and she would arrange it with the sheriff so you wouldn't get in trouble with the judge."

"I'll have to call and thank her." Looking at Silas, she lowered her pride enough to explain, "I'm afraid I don't have any friends where my things are, or I could have asked them to send me a few of my clothes. The majority of my time was spent working." Alanna felt herself turn red. Several of the men and women whom she had worked with had made attempts to become friendlier , which she had sidestepped with a variety of excuses to keep a distance between them.

She hated the thought of Silas thinking she was a total loser.

He gave her an understanding smile, which soothed her ruffled pride. "Diamond said you live in Ohio?"

"Yes."

"I don't expect the judge is going to give you a pass to leave the state anytime soon."

"No, he won't," she agreed. "When I get paid, I'll buy what I need."

"The boys are always up for a road trip. Go through the clothes Diamond gave you and make a list of items you want from your home. Ginny and the boys can go on Saturday."

"Ginny? I can't ask—"

"Ginny's been waiting to go baby shopping for a couple of weeks. This will give her an excuse to visit a big city to shop. She's having a girl this time around and wants to buy all the girly stuff she missed out on buying with Freddy."

"Still ..."

"Boys been needing a few things, too. You'd be doing them all a favor."

Dispirited, Alanna knew she had little choice but to accept their help. The more she talked with Silas, the more she was beginning to realize that on the surface, he came across as laidback and affable, yet he somehow managed to lead her in the direction he wanted her to go. The thought had her jerkily walking to the closet to disguise her reaction. She was just overreacting, she told herself, staring inside the closet at the clothes Mrs. Bates had sent her.

Something was bothering her about Silas. It was unexplainable, but there was an inkling at the back of her mind trying to get out, and the more she tried to interpret what it was trying to tell, the more the feeling retreated.

"Ginny's got dinner on the table. I hope you're hungry."

She was about to deny she was, but Silas didn't give her the opportunity to refuse.

"Ginny's been cooking all day, so you would have your choice of options," he said wryly. "She didn't want to offend you if you're vegan, or there is a type of food you don't like, so she covered her bases."

"Your sister shouldn't have gone to any trouble for me. I don't want to impose myself on your family's gatherings—"

"It's not an imposition. You can meet everyone, and I need to give you the cell phone when you're there. We won't keep you out too long, I promise." Silas motioned her toward the bedroom door.

Left with no choice other than acting like an ungrateful bitch, Alanna left the room and made her way out of the trailer. Only when they were retracing their steps to Silas' house did it dawn on her that she had given in to him again. She nearly stumbled over a protruding tree root when her subconsciousness warned her that Silas might be coming across as laidback and understanding while in reality, he was more of an iron fist in a velvet glove.

"Careful," Silas warned.

"I will ..." Righting herself, Alanna saw the outbuilding where Silas had told her his brothers worked. About to take another step forward, she was lowering her eyes back to the ground when the door of the building opened and two men came outside.

Mesmerized, Alanna forgot how to walk, freezing in place. Both men were striking to look at. It was hard not to stare when neither man wore a shirt. Faded jeans lovingly hugging their hips had her eyes jerk upward at the wayward thoughts materializing from her starved libido.

Alanna had never been the type of woman who was attracted to men with bulging muscles or rock-hard abs. Those were the ones she shied away from the most because of Owen.

She was still congratulating herself for giving the first one out the door only a brief once-over when her eyes went to the man behind him and clung like someone who had become lost in a parched desert and was dying of thirst.

He had to be a mirage. There was no man who had a face like a Greek god and was gifted with a body to match who would willingly live on a mountain, surrounded by trees instead of lying on a beach, surrounded by a variety of buxom beauties catering to his every want and need.

Locking her knees to keep from falling over flat on her face, Alanna looked up at the bright sky overhead, trying to restore the balance that had just been knocked out of her. Taking a steadying breath, she said a silent prayer in her head that her tongue would become unglued from the roof of her mouth.

Please don't let me make a fool of myself, she added before ending the prayer.

Maybe he was just a mirage ... Lowering her eyes back down from the sky, Alanna felt as if she had just been captured in a golden butterfly net. She was trapped by his gaze when a shadowy flashback had her reeling backward a step.

She was standing face to face with the man who had stood outside her cell door three days ago, and she had willingly let herself be brought right to his doorstep.

Chapter Seven

"What are you doing here?"

Alanna was shaken that who she had been starting to think was a figment of her imagination actually wasn't. The misgivings she had been experiencing since leaving the courthouse were right.

Taking her eyes off the two men standing by the building, she cast a quick glance at Silas before jerking her eyes back to the other two men. None of them seemed shocked at her abrupt question.

"I live here."

"Alanna, these are my brothers, Matthew—"

The one she had seen at the sheriff's office nodded his head at her.

"—and Isaac." Silas' voice grew reprimanding. "Matthew only told me this morning, when I was leaving, that he had gotten arrested and might have spoken to you while he was there."

Matthew made a face. "I knew the cat would be out the bag when you saw me. I hope I didn't say anything to put you off taking the job. I'm afraid I don't remember much about that night. I'd had a few too many drinks, coupled with one of Greer's greens, so I have to admit that night is kind of a blur."

The embarrassed way he was looking at her lessened the tension she was feeling.

"The deputy gave you a joint?"

Matthew laughed at her shock. "He wasn't on duty at the time."

Silas took her arm. "We're keeping the others waiting."

Isaac gave her a bashful smile. "We were going to wash up. Give us five, and we'll be there."

Alanna let Silas lead her to the house. As they passed his truck, she gave it a wistful glance.

"You don't have to worry. Matthew doesn't make it a habit to light up. He was celebrating."

"Oh ... okay." Alanna looked to where Silas' brothers were splashing water at each other from a barrel next to their building.

Silas noticed where she was staring as they walked up the steps. "Matthew and Isaac are very close. They spend the better part of the day cutting up with each other."

"I see that." Alanna felt a familiar tightening in her chest. How many times had she spent regretting not having siblings? Even now, as an adult, she would wonder if her parents had planned to have more children. Would their marriage have lasted? She mourned not only the parents whose memories grew fainter each year, but also the future they would have had if they had lived.

Silas cast her a worried glance as he grabbed the doorknob. "Ready?"

Alanna frowned at him quizzically. "Is there something I should be prepared for?"

"Only that we can be a bit overwhelming because there are so many of us."

She loosened her guard, seeing Silas wanted her to like his

family. He was making inroads in her desire to keep a professional distance between herself and all the Colemans. He was the type of brother she had always longed for.

"I've always wanted a big family. I was an only child," she told him.

"As frustrating as mine can be, I wouldn't switch places to a smaller one."

"I don't blame you."

Silas opened the door, allowing her to enter first.

Expectant faces turned as she walked inside. The sea of males all stood as one as Silas ushered her further into the room.

"Hello," she greeted them nervously.

"Hello," they all said in unison.

"I was wondering how much longer you would be. I was about to put the roast back in the oven to keep it warm."

A cheerful female voice had Alanna turning her head toward the woman she hadn't noticed standing beside the biggest table she had ever seen. Every inch of the table was filled with empty plates waiting to be filled, and the rest was taken up with the smorgasbord of dishes that had her stomach growling.

"Silas"—the woman smiled, breaking the embarrassing moment—"you better make the introductions quick. I hear your stomach growling from over here."

Flushing, Alanna gave her a thankful glance for trying to spare her feelings. "I'm afraid that was me." Placing her hand on her stomach to smother the rumbling sounds, Alanna regretted not eating the breakfast that Deputy Porter had brought her. "I was too nervous to eat breakfast this morning."

Way to go, Alanna, she scolded herself, *just blurt out that you just came from a court hearing.*

Becoming further embarrassed, she was unaware that her bottom lip started trembling.

The woman came around the table to link arms with her. "I was nervous the first time I met them, too," she confided in an overloud whisper. "I was so nervous all I wanted to eat was cranberry sauce. It's a comfort food for me."

Giving her a warm smile, the woman introduced herself, "I'm Ginny." Urging her away from the doorway, the woman pointed to the line of men that started by Silas. "That's Jody. Next to him is Jacob, then Moses, Ezra, and the youngest is our Fynn. Don't let his height fool you. He's only twelve, so if you catch him playing his computer games before his homework is done, tell Silas.

"Ginny ..." The boy gave a loud groan.

"He will play the games nonstop if we don't keep an eye on him. He's gotten good at sneaking in the other boys' homes to play their games if Silas is here." Giving her younger brother a playful glare, she released Alanna's arm to move toward the last man, whom she hadn't been introduced to yet, and took the child from his arms to settle him comfortably on her hip.

"And last, but not least," she said, giving the man a loving smile that had her catching the love apparent between the two, "my husband, Gavin. And the one chewing on his fist is Freddy."

She loved babies. If the intimidating man weren't standing so close behind them, she wouldn't have been able to hold back from touching the child.

"He's beautiful," she said softly, staring at the child wistfully and seeing she was expecting again.

"We like to think so." Ginny gave her a questioning glance. "Would you like to hold him?"

Alanna raised her eyes from the toddler to the father. At his nod, Alanna held out her arms.

Ginny gave her a curious look at the motion, but brought

the child closer to her. Alanna took the baby and settled him on her hip the same way Ginny had done.

"You've been around children." Ginny smiled, tugging her hair away from her son's clutching fingers.

Alanna smiled, too. "I was placed in a group home when my parents died. In emergencies sometimes, they would have to take in younger children until a foster parent became available. The staff would always let me hold them when they couldn't get them to stop crying." Alanna used the bib to mop up the drool sliding down Freddy's chubby arm.

"They felt safe with you," Ginny said, smoothing her son's hair down.

Alanna breathed in the baby smell of baby powder that always filled the constant void of loneliness she lived with every day. "I knew they were scared." She automatically rocked the child when he started crying after his hand slipped out of his mouth. Finding it again, he became content once again.

The door opening behind them had Alanna turning her head to see Matthew and Isaac coming inside.

"Good. Now we can eat," Ginny proclaimed.

Alanna felt herself blushing when Matthew's eyes landed on her holding the child. She could have sworn she felt her womb clenching at the way he stared at her. Burying her face in the little boy's neck, she breathed in his calming scent.

"Alanna, do you care to buckle Freddy into his highchair for me? Gavin, can you carry the roast to the table? Boys, take your seat before the food gets cold."

Relieved to have an excuse to move away from Matthew's gaze, she carried Freddy to his highchair. Making sure he was safely buckled, she didn't immediately take a seat when she was finished.

"Alanna, you can sit next to me." Silas slid a chair out from under the table.

Taking the seat, she saw Matthew sitting across the table.

He grinned, not embarrassed to be caught staring at her. "I hope you're hungry. She cooked enough to feed an army."

Alanna looked around the huge table, using the opportunity to break eye contact. "Your family is the size of one."

His expression grew serious. "We are. We protect our own."

Her eyes flew back to his, sensing a double meaning behind his words. Was Matthew warning her? Of course, he was. Why wouldn't he? She had just been released from jail, and the ankle monitor was plainly visible.

Biting her bottom lip, she hastily looked down at her empty plate. "I would never do anything to break the trust Silas has given me."

"Alanna, look at me."

Matthew's firm voice had her lifting her eyes.

"I didn't mean it the way you took it." His demeanor held the same graveness he had shown outside her cell. "I want you to feel safe here. No one enters our property without our approval. After dinner, Moses will introduce you to his dogs so they can get your scent. Anyone who takes a step on our property uninvited won't get far before they will find themselves climbing a tree to escape them."

"Don't scare her." Silas handed her a plate of pork chops. "Don't worry. Moses trains dogs for a living. Once they have your scent, you'll never know they're around."

Alanna handed the platter of pork chops to Fynn, who had taken the seat next to her, before she glanced at the dog lying contently in front of the fireplace.

"Suki is Gavin's dog," Silas told her, passing her a basket of biscuits.

Several minutes passed with her filling her plate. Remaining quiet, she started to eat, not listening to the conversations going on between the siblings. Covertly, she studied them as she ate. None on them really resembled each other. Matthew and Isaac were brawnier than their brothers. Silas and Moses were leaner, while Jacob was more muscular. Their hair varied in color, also.

"Go ahead and ask." Matthew's lips curled in amusement.

"Excuse me?" Aware she had been caught staring, she nearly choked on a bite of food.

"None of us really look alike. That's because we each have different mothers."

Her eyes widened, and then she moved her gaze around the table, her mind working even though Silas had told her how many siblings he had.

"Your dad was married eight times?" Alanna managed to choke out, covering her mouth with a napkin.

"He was a very loving man," Ginny said hotly when the whole table broke into laughter.

"He was that." Matthew nodded in agreement. "But he didn't marry any of our eight mothers."

"Eight?" Alanna lowered her napkin.

"I'm adopted," Ginny explained with sad eyes. "We had a sister, Leah, who died when she was younger. Leah and Ezra share the same mother."

"I'm so sorry for your loss."

Matthew's pain-filled expression had her wanting to console him.

"We lost Dad and Leah at the same time. It was rough going for a while, but it's getting better. Little Freddy reminds us a lot of Dad."

"Let's hope he doesn't take after him in at least one trait," Gavin spoke for the first time since she had come into the house.

Alanna felt her lips twitching in amusement at the wry way Gavin was staring at his innocent son.

"Gavin swears he's going to watch Freddy like a hawk."

"I think you're in trouble." Alanna couldn't resist teasing

the grim man. Then something occurred her to as soon as she said it. "Freddy is the only grandchild?"

"So far. We're expecting another in the summer."

Other than Fynn, all the other Colemans were old enough to have started their own families.

"You have a question?" Matthew saw the question she was too embarrassed to ask.

"No." Reaching for her fork, she shoved a mouthful of food into her mouth to keep it busy.

"Don't be embarrassed."

Her groin started clenching at the way he looked at her.

"None of my brothers or I have tried to keep up with our dad's record."

"It's none of my business," she managed to get out.

"You didn't have to. Everyone expected us to follow in his footsteps where women were concerned. So far, they've been disappointed that their predictions haven't come true. None of us are evening dating anyone."

Alanna couldn't believe what he was telling her. There was no way that eight men looking the way these men looked, and not a one of them had a girlfriend.

Alanna looked at Ginny, thinking she would stop the men from pulling her leg. "He's joking?"

Ginny shook her head. "Matthew's telling the truth. None of them have dated."

"Why not?" She waited for the punchline, still not believing. Piercing a broccoli spear with her fork, she looked up to see Matthew staring at her intently.

"We're waiting for our soul mates."

Chapter Eight

The silence at the table became palpable after he disclosed the truth.

Matthew ignored the kick under the table that Isaac gave him, not removing his gaze from Alanna's.

"Yes ... well ..."

From the way she was looking around the table, she thought he was teasing her. He wasn't. He had never been more serious in his life.

"I don't believe I've ever heard a man waiting for their soul mate."

Silas cleared his throat. "Here. Try the sweet potatoes." Passing the potatoes to Alanna, Silas shot Matthew a warning glance.

Matthew resumed eating the food that tasted like cardboard.

"Gavin is my soul mate." Ginny laid her hand on Gavin's arm. "We're very happy. My brothers are determined to outdo me." Ginny playfully nudged Gavin with her shoulder. "He didn't believe in soul mates, either. I had to educate him. Took me a while, but I think he does now. Either that, or he's just pacifying me," she teased.

Matthew gave his sister a grateful smile, trying not to break into laughter at Gavin's reaction at finding himself being pulled off the sideline.

"We're soul mates." Gavin said, giving his wife a threatening glance for putting him on the spot.

Matthew finally was able to enjoy the food on his plate. Misery does love company.

Gavin's embarrassment was nothing like the misery he had been dealing with since he had seen Alanna. All he had wanted to do when he came out of his shop and saw her was pick her up, carry her to his trailer, lock the door, and never let her leave.

Reaching for his glass of tea, he had to steady his hand before picking it up.

Waiting for Alanna had tested his endurance. It was only the repercussions that his family would be punished with that had prevented him from making an opportunity to insert himself in her life before the stars had determined they would meet.

He had to tell himself that he wasn't the only one suffering from waiting. All his brothers were waiting for their time to come. Some, like Isaac and him, were near their breaking points, while Ezra and Fynn were still settling into the fact that their hearts were meant for a certain girl.

Matthew sympathized with them. While he hadn't fought having a soul mate, Isaac hadn't given in easily. Each of his brothers dealt the hand they had been given by the stars differently. Silas, Moses, and he were waiting for their soul mates. Isaac, Jody, and Ezra had tried to beat the stars by being with women other than their soul mates. Jody and Ezra had quickly stopped. Matthew hadn't asked why, nor did he want to know. He could see the regret in their eyes.

Isaac was different; he always had been. Out of all his brothers, he was the closest to Isaac, yet in other ways, he was the least like him. Isaac walked in the shadow world, and each time he did, Matthew was afraid he wouldn't return.

"Only a child as beautiful as Freddy could have been created by that type of special bond."

Matthew was staring at Alanna when she started talking, and the love he felt for her deepened. He didn't have to look at Ginny to see Alanna had stolen her heart as well.

"Thank you." Ginny scooted the platter of roast beef closer to her.

Alanna shook her head. "If I eat any more, I'm going to burst."

Ginny began to look upset. "You haven't eaten dessert." Rising from the table, she went into the kitchen then returned with a strawberry truffle.

Matthew hid his smile when Alanna took one look at the truffle and her eyes widened in pleasure.

"I love strawberries."

His sister beamed as she passed out dessert plates. "Silas, do you mind getting the coffee pot?"

Silas went to the kitchen, bringing the coffee pot and holding a cell phone in his other hand. "I'll set up the cell phone for you."

Matthew watched as Silas took his seat again while Ginny scooped out a generous serving of the truffle onto Alanna's plate.

"Can I have a little more?" she asked, not taking her plate back. "Strawberry truffle is my favorite dessert."

Ginny gave her another generous scoop.

"Thank you." Blushing, Alanna set her dessert plate down then immediately speared a fork into a huge strawberry with a dollop of whipped cream. She licked the whipped cream off before eating the fruit.

Imagining her licking something else, he didn't pay attention to Ginny filling his plate.

Nudging his shoulder with her hip, Ginny forced him back to awareness at the hungry way he was watching Alanna.

Everyone at the table started making exaggerated efforts to eat their strawberries in a way that made fun of him staring at her. After giving each of his brothers threatening glares, he kept his gaze downcast on his own plate.

"Here you go, Ginny," Silas said, giving the cell phone to Ginny. "You can put yours and Gavin's cell phone number in then pass it down."

Silas turned his attention to Alanna. "Tomorrow morning, Ginny will walk you around the rest of the property, show you the jobs you'll be taking over for her. You can start work on Monday."

"But ... that's three days away. I can work this weekend," Alanna protested.

"Monday is soon enough. Your salary is for Monday through Friday. Tomorrow isn't a day off. By the time she gets done showing you around, you'll need Friday off. You can also use Friday to make a list of what you want from your home so Ginny can pack for you."

He turned his attention to his sister. "Matthew and Isaac volunteered to drive you. They know you've been wanting to go shopping."

"You don't have to." Alanna glanced at Ginny worriedly. "I don't want to put any of you out. I can make do—"

"You'll be doing her a favor." It was Gavin who put an end to her protests. "She's been asking me to take her. It will give me and Freddy a boys' day."

Unlike with Silas, Alanna didn't argue with Gavin. The quick darts of fear she kept casting in Gavin's direction showed she was afraid of him.

"I'll do the dishes." Getting up from the table, Alanna started picking up the dirty dishes.

"Leave them. It's Fynn and Jody's turn." Matthew stood up from the table to take the dishes away from her. "Isaac, key in my number for her," he said from over his shoulder as he carried the dishes to the sink.

When he walked out of the kitchen, he saw Alanna heading out the front door with Moses, Gavin, and Ginny carrying Freddy. Rushing forward, he was following Ginny when Silas pulled him back, shutting the door.

"Gavin and Ginny are going to walk her back to the trailer."

Matthew shook Silas' hand off his arm. "I'm walking her—"

"No, you're not." Silas maneuvered in front of the door, blocking him from leaving.

"Move, Silas."

"No. You'll scare her off if you come on too strong. After she saw you, I was afraid she would go for the truck instead of coming in the front door. Don't lose your shit when you're so close to having it all."

His jaw jutted out stubbornly. "Move ... I just want to talk to her a little longer."

Isaac, Jody, Ezra, and Fynn moved in front of Silas.

Isaac raised a brow at him. "We both know you're wanting more than talking. If Silas can act normal in front of his woman for years, then you can, too, for a few weeks until she gets to know you better."

"She knows me."

"She thinks you're a figment of her imagination. She thinks we both are," Silas said from behind his brothers. "You didn't see her face when she realized you were in jail with her. You missed how she wouldn't take Freddy from Ginny until she moved away from Gavin." Silas gave a deep sigh. "Once she gets comfortable with you and the rest of us, it will be easier to tell her."

"How is she going to get comfortable with me when you won't even let me walk her to the trailer?" Matthew ran a trembling hand over his closely cut hair.

"I didn't say you couldn't be around her, just not tonight. Your emotions are all over the place. Hell, I thought you were going to jump over the table when she was eating dessert."

Storming toward the couch, he threw himself down irritably. Knowing his brother was right didn't make admitting it any easier.

"This sucks," he groaned, burying his head in his hands.

"Fynn, Ezra, you can get started on the dishes," Silas ordered.

Matthew felt the couch sink down next to him. Then Silas laid a comforting a hand on his back. "It could be worse."

"How?" Matthew lifted his head to glare at his older brother.

Silas watched Fynn leave the room before giving him a sly grin. "You might have blue balls, but at least you don't have a case of morning sickness, like Ginny usually does," he said meaningfully.

Matthew frowned, thinking Silas had lost it. Then realization dawned. Reaching his hand down to the side, he pulled down the lever to raise the recliner.

"You want to watch the game?" He couldn't bear another lonely night alone in his trailer, not when Alanna was just steps away from his.

Silas gave him another pat, getting up. "I'll get the beer."

Isaac sat down across from him on the other couch, making himself comfortable. "Grab me one, too." Isaac threw a smirk in his direction. "And can you get me some more of that strawberry truffle? Make sure you put plenty—"

Matthew didn't let Isaac finish what he was about to say. He couldn't. A fist was blocking his airway.

Chapter Nine

Matthew looked at the time on his cell phone. Was eight too early? Unable to take pacing around his trailer another second, he went outside.

Taking a steadying breath, he made his way to Silas' house. After pouring himself a cup of coffee, he unloaded the dishwasher that Fynn and Ezra had started last night. It would be one of the jobs which would be given to Alanna once she started work. The simple job was one that had become habit for all the brothers when they stopped by the house. They all pitched in to do the main house chores so Silas could come into a clean house. Their older brother did the majority of the work on the mountain, only pulling them off their pursuits when he needed their help.

Pouring another cup in a thermos, he started a new pot. Silas would start the first pot of the day when he woke up, normally around six. Throughout the day, several other pots would be made by whomever emptied the last.

His brothers and he all had their own coffee pots, but it was a habit to come by Silass's—his tasted better. He didn't know why, since they had the same coffee setup as Silas.

Glancing at the time on the coffeemaker, Matthew carried his coffee cup and the thermos outside, heading toward Jody's trailer. From the smoke coming out of the workshop, Isaac was finishing up the order for an iron gate they were scheduled to set up on Monday.

His heart started pumping hard as he approached the trailer where Alanna was staying. Placing the extra thermos in the crook of his other arm, he ran his hand over hair. He had gotten a trim just the day before yesterday. Alanna preferred men with shorter hair.

Knocking on the door, he anxiously waited for her to answer. When she didn't answer immediately, he frowned, knocking again. He was about to pull out his cell phone to call her when the door was jerked open to reveal a groggy Alanna holding a shoe in her hand.

"Sorry. I overslept." Craning her neck to look over his shoulder, she held the edge of the door, as if ready to shut it in his face. "I hope your sister hasn't been waiting for me."

"Ginny is under the weather, so she called and asked me to show you around. She should be feeling better by the time we make it to her house."

"Oh ... okay. Just give me a second to put my shoe on."

Matthew raised an eyebrow when she closed the door. *What the fuck? Does she think I'm going to jump her if she lets me inside?*

Moving off the steps, he waited for her to come out.

She's just nervous, like I am, he thought to himself, giving her a reassuring smile when she came out.

"Sorry to keep you waiting, I had trouble sleeping. I kept hearing things moving around outside. I live in a high rise, so being out here in the wilderness will take some getting used to."

She considers this the wilderness? Maybe it was, and he was so used to it that he was wrong.

"You're good. We can get started at Silas' home, and I can show you the chores there then move along to the rest of the places."

"Okay."

"I brought you some coffee." He started to hand her the thermos.

"No, thank you. I don't drink coffee."

Since when?

Alanna reached out to take it from him. "I can carry it, though."

"I can."

So, she quit drinking coffee. He mentally shrugged. Why did he care? Because he had counted on knowing every one of her likes and dislikes to further getting her comfortable with him. He had waited so long for her. He had hoped being familiar with things she liked would be sort of a shortcut for him.

Silas had done him a favor by stopping him from walking her home. He could have fucked himself over by saying the wrong thing.

Seeking to put her at ease, he started talking. "The sounds you heard were probably raccoons or possums. They come out at night. Don't worry; they are more afraid of you than you will be of them. Just bang a pot, and they take off."

"Can they get inside the trailer?"

"No," he assured her, seeing the worry in her gaze.

Reaching Silas' house, he held the door open for her. Seeing her hesitation, he stepped back from the door so she wouldn't have to brush past him. The woman was more skittish than a cat around a pack of dogs.

Going inside, he directed her to the kitchen, letting her go first, keeping a couple of steps behind her.

"Your sister cooked the huge meal we ate yesterday in this kitchen?"

Matthew frowned at her shocked expression. "Yes. Why?"

"Nothing. It's just smaller than I expected," she said, looking around the kitchen.

"Silas has been wanting to redo it, but he decided to wait and let who he marries do it the way she wants."

Alanna gave him amused smile. "He's dating someone?"

Does she think I was lying yesterday?

"No."

"He's waiting for his soul mate, too?"

Matthew could tell she didn't believe him for a hot second.

Afraid of coming off as creepy, he distracted her by showing her how to refill the coffee machine. "When this light turns red, the machine needs to be cleaned." After showing her under the counter where the cleaning supplies were for the machine, he then made a new pot before pouring the coffee he had made for her down the drain.

"I didn't mean for it to go to waste," she said, noticing what he was doing. "I thought you would drink it."

"I don't take creamer and sugar." Washing the thermos out, he dried it before putting it back in the cabinet.

"How did you know how I used to drink my coffee?"

"Don't most women drink it with sugar and creamer?" Opening the freezer drawer, he hid his expression as he took out two packs of frozen hamburger meat, which had already been cooked in a large batch then separated out into one-pound serving sizes.

"Silas usually leaves the house at six. The main chore you will be responsible for is to unload the dishwasher, make sure there is enough coffee made for whoever comes over, and start dinner for Silas. If anyone comes here before you, the dishwasher will already be unloaded. It's a habit we've had since we were kids. Each of us takes turns loading the dishwasher the night before, depending who comes by to eat with Silas."

"The dishwasher was already unloaded. Someone has already been here?"

"I was. We all get a pretty early start. We all come by to get coffee and make sure Fynn hasn't missed the school bus."

Alanna nodded. "I'll make sure I get here early, then."

"You can set your own schedule. Ginny does. We'll let you start the meal. We hate that chore. The only difference would be whether to set it on low or high, depending what time you get here."

Matthew pointed at a white plastic maker board hanging on the pantry door. Days of the week had been written out with the meals underneath.

"Tonight is chili. All you have to do is"—Matthew opened a drawer under the Crock-Pot to take out a three-ring note-book—"flip to chili and follow the directions."

Matthew expected her to come closer to look at the note-book. When she didn't, he stepped away to give her space.

"The seasoning packets and can ingredients are in the pantry." Taking two steps to the side, he opened the large pantry, which held a deep freezer. When she didn't come inside, he gathered the ingredients himself and carried them to the counter, making sure to give her enough space. He then put the ingredients into the crockpot. Hitting the button, he turned to see she was standing by the doorway. Disposing of the trash and recycling the cans, he turned toward her.

"We're done here... We'll go on to Isaac's trailer."

Alanna frowned at him. "I don't need to do something else before I leave?"

"Nope, that's pretty much all. Silas takes the trash out in the morning, and Fynn does his breakfast dishes and puts them away."

She was out of the front door before he could make it through the dining room.

What the fuck is going on with her?

Determined to be upbeat, he tried to draw her into a conversation. He pointed out where Isaac and he worked, only to be told Silas had already told her. Each time he tried to talk to her, she would lag behind him until he felt he was talking to himself.

In Isaac's house, there wasn't much to show her. He must have done a deep clean in preparation of Alanna coming.

"Isaac will leave a note if he needs a chore done. Looks like all he needed today was a couple of steaks brought from the main freezer. I can bring them on my way back to my place."

Alanna stared around the house that Isaac and he had bought online and built together.

She left the kitchen and explored the rest of the house, coming back with a frown. "He didn't even leave me the bed to make."

"We're used to being self-proficient."

Leaving Isaac's, he took to Jacob's.

"All they need is for you to put the clothes in the dryer and get laundry detergent from the storeroom. I'll drop it off."

Coming out of Jacob's second-hand trailer, he led her through a heavily wooded area.

As they neared the end, he stopped and reached out to take her arm. She had been following him with her head down and seen he had stopped. At his touch, she jerked her arm away, lifting frightened eyes to his.

"I was just trying ..." he began when she rushed forward.

"Alanna, stop!" Running, he barely managed to catch her around her waist.

"Don't touch me!" she screamed, hitting him on the hand looped around her waist. "Don't ever put your filthy hands on me!"

Containing her struggles, he walked backward with her then turned again so she could get a better view.

"Look." Shaking her to get her to stop fighting him, he got

a firm hold on her with one hand before jerking her head down. "You would have fallen if I hadn't stopped you."

Chapter Ten

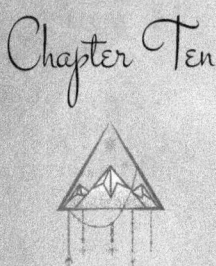

Forcing herself to look, Alanna saw she would have gone over the edge of a steep hill. Below were a house, paddock, and two metal buildings.

"I'm sorry. Thank you. I reacted badly ..." she managed to choke out, feeling his hands drop away from her.

"It's okay. I should have warned you that we were coming to a drop-off."

Alanna bit her lip at the stiff way he had spoken to her.

"Here's how we get down." Matthew started going down the path.

She didn't have to walk slowly behind him to keep him from talking to her; he had stopped. Nor did he turn around to see if she was having any problem coming down the hill.

Alanna wanted to burst into tears at the hurt look she had seen on his face when she had screamed at him.

At the bottom, he went inside one of the buildings, not waiting for her.

She walked to the door and saw him turning on the light. Coming farther inside, she then watched as he strode toward several freezers.

"On top of the freezer is a list of what is inside. When you take something out, mark it so Silas can track of what he needs to buy." Opening one freezer, Matthew took out two steaks before closing it. He reached for the ink pen hanging on the wall, and she saw him writing on the paper.

She glanced around the building; it reminded her of a small store, with the different shelves holding a variety of items.

Matthew disappeared behind one shelving unit to return with a bottle of detergent. Coming to a stop by the freezer, he paused. "We can go on to the other building."

When she didn't move, and he didn't either, she realized he was waiting for her to move from the doorway. Blushing, she stepped back. He was plainly showing her that the message she had intentionally been giving him this morning had been received.

Isn't this what you wanted? She had deliberately set out to keep their conversation on employee and employer terms, so why did she feel as if she had just ruined something special? Expecting to have a difficult day after a nearly sleepless night had been proven to be true. Still, she would never have guessed just how badly she had flubbed it up.

"Ginny should be feeling better by now," he said, walking away from the building.

"What's in the other building?" She hurried after him.

"Feed for the goats. Ginny will show you," he muttered without turning his head.

Alanna attempted to breach the gap she had created. "Who lives in the house?"

"Moses. You don't have to do anything at his house."

Walking past Moses's house, they went up a steeper incline with a well-worn path.

"Is it safe for your sister to walk this in her condition?"

"She uses her car. There's a back road that goes around the

mountain, to the goat pen and storage buildings. There's a golf cart, too, which is in the other building. If you don't want to walk, you can ask him for the keys. He'll have to sit with you while he teaches you how to drive it," he warned.

Alanna winced at the shot he just fired at her. *Wow, way to go, Alanna.*

The way she'd been acting, she wouldn't have shown her either.

"Her place is just ahead. She can drive you back to the Silas' house after she shows you what chores she needs done."

"What's your sister's last name?"

Her question had Matthew stopping to stare at her. "Why?"

"So I'll know how to address her."

His brow furrowed. "You call her Ginny, like we all do."

"I prefer to keep everything on a last name basis."

"Then ask her yourself."

She was doing a bang-up job so far. She would be lucky to keep the job by Monday with the way she kept putting her foot in her mouth.

There was no way she could explain to Matthew the nightmares that had plagued her mind from her childhood. From all outward appearances, she seemed to be a well-adjusted, normal adult. Instead, she was anything but.

She had talked to two, not just one, voices in her head when she was growing up, and she had constant nightmares where she was hiding from Kate and Owen. She had taken her medication last night, so it would take at least a couple of nights for the nightmares to be buffered enough for her to get a restful night's sleep.

Rounding a huge oak tree, she was treated with the first sight of Ginny's home. It was a larger version of Silas' home.

Walking to the front door, Alanna expected Matthew to knock. Instead, he went inside, leaving her to follow.

Slowly entering the room, she saw Ginny sitting on a leather couch, watching Freddy play on the floor.

Ginny noticed her standing in the doorway. "Come on in. Sorry about this morning." Ginny raised the cup she was holding. "Morning sickness. I've had a cup of tea, so I'm good to go.

"Matthew, do you mind watching Freddy while I show Alanna around?"

Alanna smiled when Matthew dropped down on the floor and began playing with the baby.

"Matthew is Freddy's favorite uncle. My other brothers get bored when I ask them to watch him. Matthew would keep him if Gavin and I would let him.

Taking in Ginny's home as they went toward the kitchen off from the living room, Alanna appreciated how you could still look directly into the other room. While the outside might look like Silas', the inside was modern. The kitchen had two ovens, two dishwashers, and two microwaves, all with high-end appliances that a cook could only dream about.

"Your home is lovely," Alanna complimented her.

"Thank you. We only finished rebuilding it a couple of months ago."

"Rebuilt? It looks brand new."

"We had started this house in another section of the property. This area was meant for Leah. The one meant for me had an explosion, so Silas gave me Leah's. The area that was damaged, as well as the cow pens, Silas and my brothers are slowly clearing out so they can regrow the trees they have to pull down."

Alanna took her eyes off the glass refrigerator she had only seen in stores. "What kind of explosion?"

Ginny sighed. "I might as well tell you. All you have to do is ask around town, and they'll fill you in. My mother bombed my house. Instead of offing me, she was caught in the blast herself. I had left. I didn't know until I had gone to The Last Riders' house and they looked at me like I was a ghost."

Alanna stiffened at the mention of the bikers. "You know The Last Riders?"

"Yes, I do. I used to work for them. I'm friends with them." Ginny grew curious at her expression. "Have you heard of them?"

Alanna stared at her stonily. "The Last Riders are how I ended up in jail."

Chapter Eleven

"The Last Riders aren't the reason why you were in jail."

Her breath became lodged in her throat at seeing Gavin standing in the doorway off from the living room.

"You're right. I apologize." Alanna managed to get enough oxygen to get the words out. "I have no one else to blame, but myself. Being in jail wasn't an experience I want to relive. I think I've developed PTSD from being there. Take it from me; you don't want to end up there. I would rather go to maximum security prison."

"It was that bad?" Ginny asked sympathetically.

She wasn't aware she was shaking until Ginny looped her arm through hers to give her a steadying strength.

"They kept the temperature at minus zero, Deputy Porter would use any excuse to talk to me for hours on end, and he would pick and choose what food I would eat for the day then confiscate some of it whenever he wanted it for himself. Once I get my charges dropped, I'm going to file a suit against the jail for inhumane treatment."

Never in her life had she ever wanted to melt into the floor as she did with the way Matthew, Gavin, and Ginny were staring at her as she finally finished the rant she had been holding in since her release.

Alanna brought her hand to face. "I have never been so embarrassed in my life. Ignore everything I—"

Laughter bubbled out from Ginny. Alanna looked through splayed fingers to see Gavin, whose expression had been deadpanning the short time she had met him, had amusement curling his lips. Even Matthew's frosty behavior had thawed enough to show he was holding back his own laughter.

"Uh ... I hate to tell you this"—Ginny chocked back her laughter—"but Greer treats everyone the same way, regardless if you're in jail or not. He's been kicked out of every restaurant in town. King has threatened two lawsuits, and the owner of the burger place in town locks the door when he sees him crossing the street toward his place."

Alanna let her hand fall back to her side. "Then I don't understand. Why doesn't someone sue him, or at least have him fired from the sheriff's office?"

They all stopped laughing.

Gavin's expression went deadpan again. "Because everyone in town knows that, as irritating as Greer is, there isn't a person in town he wouldn't risk his life for and, in fact, has."

Alanna stared at him doubtfully. "He has?"

"He has. I'm actually one of them."

Dammit. Alanna raised her eyes up heavenward. *Did I not ask You not to let me make a fool of myself? So far, You're failing massively.* Criticizing God might not be the smart way to go, but how much worse could it be? She had probably alienated half of the Colemans with her behavior.

"I just can't understand his fascination with food."

"Probably because he didn't have much when he was a kid." Matthew raised Freddy to sit on top of his knees and started pretending to buck him off as he talked. "Silas told us. Greer and Silas are the same age. They were even in school together. He said Greer's family only had food to eat from their mother's garden and what meat they raised. They would practically starve in the winter when their canned food ran out. Greer's father made what money they had by moonshining, which wasn't much because most of what he made, he drank. His mother would take a beating if she got caught taking charity from any of the townspeople. Silas said the first new shoes Greer had ever gotten, he had stolen from him."

Each word Matthew said just hammered another nail in her coffin.

"Greer stole Silas' shoes?" Alanna's hopes began to rise. Greer stealing Silas' shoes showed he wasn't nice, didn't it? "He shouldn't have stolen from Silas."

Matthew gave her a rueful look. "Silas had been bullying Greer. It was payback."

"Probably self-preservation," she muttered. She didn't believe Silas was bullying Greer without a just cause.

Ginny and Gavin nodded, agreeing with her.

"We think that's why Greer did it, too."

She had meant Silas probably had bullied Greer out of self-preservation, but she had made enough bad impressions for the day. Ginny and Gavin might have assumed that was what she meant, but from Matthew's expression, he knew exactly who she was talking about.

Alanna cleared her throat. "Can we just start over?" Looking around the spick-and-span kitchen, she then gazed questioningly at Ginny. "What chores are you needing done?"

Ginny turned red. "I'm hoping you don't consider it a chore. What would be a lifesaver for me is at twelve, you two you could stop by and babysit Freddy for me while I take a nap? That's the time of day I get the sleepiest, and I won't have to ask Gavin to stop what he's doing to come back to the house."

Alanna's jaw dropped. Snapping it back, she saw they had taken her shocked reaction the wrong way.

She hastily explained, "I wouldn't consider babysitting Freddy a chore. I would love to babysit Freddy. I don't even need to be paid." She grinned at them. "I would pay you to be able to."

Ginny's face broke into a beautiful smile, which reminded her of Freddy. "I wouldn't go that far if I were you. Even though I am his mother, I think he's really easy to watch. He's been a perfect angel since we've had him."

"I can start today."

Ginny shook her head, bursting Alanna's bubble of happiness. "Gavin's off the next two days, and he called dibs on Saturday. Sunday is Silas' day; he devotes the whole day to Freddy."

Matthew rose, lifting Freddy into his arms. "If you had said something, Isaac and I would have taken turns coming by at that time."

Ginny made a face at him. "Which is why I didn't say anything. You're having trouble filling your orders now, without me taking part of your day. Besides, it was Silas' idea to hire someone who can make it easier on all of us. That way, I don't feel so guilty for hiring someone just for a couple of hours a day."

"I wouldn't have been hired either. I would still be in jail if Silas hadn't been looking to hire someone." Alanna came from behind the kitchen counter to where Matthew was standing.

"May I?" Holding her arms to Freddy, she lifted the toddler out of Matthew's hold at his nod. Settling Freddy on her hip, she felt the first peace of mind she had felt all day. "Anytime you feel like you need a break, I wouldn't mind watching him. Mr. Coleman said you weren't feeling well this morning."

Ginny grimaced. "I've been having a terrible time with morning sickness."

"I could come over here after going to Silas' house and doing the chores he needs done there, get Freddy up, dressed, and feed him breakfast. By then, your morning sickness will be better."

Neither Gavin nor Ginny seemed opposed to the idea.

"How about the mornings I'm not feeling well, I'll text you. I prefer being here myself to take care of Ginny, but I've been going out on jobs with Matthew and Isaac. That way, those days I'm scheduled to go with them, I don't have to call out to them."

Alanna smiled at the couple. "Works for me."

"Since you're feeling better, Ginny, I'm going to take off." Matthew reached out toward Freddy. "See you later, sprout. Gavin, I'll see you at the shop when you're ready."

Alanna flushed, not missing the way Matthew pulled his hand away from touching Freddy while she was holding him.

After Matthew left, she was aware of Gavin and Ginny staring at her curiously.

Ginny broke the uncomfortable silence. "Gavin, if you watch Freddy, I can take Alanna to teach her how to milk the goats and show her the rest of the houses that Matthew didn't."

Alanna relinquished Freddy to his mother's hold.

"No problem. They don't need me until three. Take your time."

Attempting to get back on even footing by reminding herself that she couldn't be friends with them, she had to tell herself that their diminished friendliness was a plus.

"I'm excited about learning how to milk a goat."

Gavin gave her a mocking glance. "Have you been around goats before?"

"No, sadly. I've never had the opportunity to be around many animals."

"Then buckle up. You're in for a treat."

Alanna frowned after Gavin when he left without another word, leaving her alone with Ginny.

Seeing she was staring after Gavin curiously, Ginny shrugged. "Gavin has had issues with the goats."

She frowned. "What issues?"

Ginny grinned. "He's a man."

Chapter Twelve

Alanna took one look in the mirror when she arrived back in the trailer and burst into tears. The Benadryl she had been given hadn't eased the swollen distortion of her eyes, nose, and lips. How had she not known she was allergic to some types of animal fur?

Everything had been going well when Ginny had taken her back to the paddock and Silas had brought the herd of goats. They were still chomping on the twigs that they had carried from the land they were clearing. Silas hadn't stayed long.

One glance, and she had fallen in love with the smaller goats trotting behind their mothers. For the fifteen minutes Ginny had shown her how to separate a particular goat from the herd then load it into a protective chute, everything went well. It was only when they were loading the third goat into the chute that she had become aware of Ginny staring at her strangely.

"Alanna, I don't want to alarm you, but I think you're having an allergic reaction."

She was reaching over her shoulder, scratching, when she turned to Ginny, who couldn't hide her aghast expression.

"Get in the car while I release Nelly back into the pen. I'll be right behind you."

She started scratching the side of her jaw. "Where are we going?"

"To the ER."

Ginny drove her to the ER with her on the phone with the sheriff, explaining why her ankle monitor was going off. The sheriff was waiting at the emergency room entrance when they arrived and stayed with her during the doctor's treatment. Alanna stared fixedly ahead, sitting on the exam table each time a new orderly or nurse entered the cubicle. Even the sheriff had started snapping at them for the made-up excuses they gave for entering. If she hadn't been aware of small-town gossip before, she was before being released.

By the time she was back in Ginny's car, the tiny fraction of pride she had left was put in a dumpster and set on fire when Deputy Porter parked behind them before Ginny could pull out. Alanna hid her face and refused to roll the window down when Greer knocked on her window. Ginny got out the car, explaining to him that Alanna wasn't feeling well. Despite another attempt to get her to roll the window down, the deputy gave up when the sheriff ordered him back to the office.

Once back at Silas', Ginny had walked her back to the trailer and wanted to come in with her.

"Thank you, Ginny, but I'm just going to sleep this medicine off. I'll be fine."

"Let me stay. The doctor didn't want you left alone," she had argued. "I'll be as quiet as a mouse and sit in the living room."

"The swelling is starting to go down. I can feel my lips again." Alanna hadn't mentioned she just wanted to be left alone.

Disbelief had shown on her face. "Are you sure? I really don't want to leave."

"I'm sure. I'll even text you once an hour if that makes you less worried."

"Promise?"

"I promise." Alanna would have given her a reassuring smile, but it hurt too bad.

She had finally convinced Ginny to leave.

Wetting a cloth, she wiped the stinging tears away. Holding the cold cloth to her face, she was about to come out of the bathroom when she heard a firm knock on her door.

She reluctantly headed to the door. She was afraid if she didn't answer, whoever was outside would come inside to check on her.

Standing behind the door, she only cracked it a small amount to peer outside.

Silas' compassionate eyes stared back at hers.

"You might as well come out. I'm not leaving until I see the damage."

She didn't have any fight left in her after she had looked at herself in the mirror. Opening the door, she pulled the cloth away from her face.

"Not as bad as I expected. I saw worse when Jody got stung by hornets. He survived. The swelling seems to be going down. I guess you milking the goats will be off your to-do list," he teased.

"I feel terrible that the job you needed me for the most, I won't even be able to do. I'll understand if you need to hire someone else," she told him numbly.

"Milking the goats wasn't the main job I hired you for. Worse comes to worst, I can milk the ornery things myself. What I need you the most for is to give Ginny a hand with Freddy. Are you allergic to him?"

"No." Alanna winced when she tried to smile at his teasing.

"Then we're good."

Alanna sniffed something in the air.

"I just put some steaks on the firepit before coming here. Want to keep me company while I finish grilling them? There might be a steak in it for you."

"I couldn't impose ..." She shook her head, not wanting anyone to see her, especially Matthew.

"No imposition. The boys won't be back until late. All the boys are at the Hardy's to set their fence and gate. Al didn't want them to set it without him being there, so they had to wait until he got off work. You could wash the potatoes for me, so I don't have to take my eyes off the steaks."

Alanna couldn't resist; the smell was driving her crazy. "You win. I'm starving."

"Then let's get you fed."

Walking to the firepit didn't take long. Alanna had seen it yesterday when Silas had taken her to the trailer. As she stared at the huge number of steaks on the grill, her mouth began to water.

"How many potatoes do you want me to wash?"

"Twenty should be enough in case any of them want seconds."

"Or thirds," she joked. "What do I do with them after I wash them?"

"Bring them here and the foil from the pantry. I'll bury them in the ash."

"Oh ..." she said excitedly. "I've never had them that way before."

"First time for everything."

Alanna nodded, turned toward the house, then paused. "You don't happen to have marshmallows, do you?"

"I do." Silas grinned. "You'll find them in the pantry.

There are graham crackers there, too. And if you look under the drawer in the refrigerator, you'll find some chocolate bars."

"I don't want to put you to trouble."

"No trouble. You can make them."

"Deal." Alanna rushed off, anxious to toast marshmallows. She'd never done it before over a fire.

Quickly washing the potatoes, she put them in a large bowl then gathered up the rest of the other items she needed.

When she came back, she saw Silas had put out two folding chairs near the firepit and placed a folding table within reach.

She set the items down, and they got busy wrapping the potatoes, then he showed her how he buried them in the hot ashes.

When she went to do one, he wouldn't let her.

"I think you've had enough mishaps for the day. If you want to help, you could gather up a few sticks for the marshmallows."

"I can do that. What size should I get?"

Silas showed her the desired length, and she was lucky enough to find a cluster of sticks sitting not far away. That was when she saw something.

Staring at the structure hidden behind a mass of vines, she wondered what it was supposed to be.

Returning to the firepit, she asked Silas.

"You must be talking about the old fort Dad built for us boys to keep us out of his hair. We used to love playing there. Even when we got older, we would sneak out to spend the night there until Leah and Ginny stole it from us, making it a pretend cabin, and they had to save their dolls and stuffed animals from grizzly bears and wolves."

Ginny moved her chair closer to the firepit. "Not possums or raccoons?"

"No, and those are what they should have been watching

out for. Popeye stole Ginny's favorite doll. I had to spend two days looking for it."

"A one-eye raccoon, who was the bane of my father's existence for many years. He loved to turn our trash cans over if one of us boys forgot to place a big rock on top when we took the trash out at night."

Alanna laughed. "Were you able to find the doll?"

"No, but we did have a memorial service for Minnie."

She laughed so hard that she had to hold her stomach. "I bet it was nice growing up with so many brothers and sisters."

"It was. Do you plan on having a large family?"

Alanna sobered instantly. "No. I never plan to have children."

"Do you mind me asking why? I saw you holding Freddy. You seem to have a natural affinity to them."

"My parents died when I was young. I'll never take a chance that I'll leave a child the way I was left."

"I'm sure they didn't want to."

"They might not have, but they didn't take any precautions either. My parents went into an area marked 'do not enter,' nor did they make arrangements for my care if anything happened to them."

"Both correctable mistakes, which you would be more cautious about, to make sure that didn't happen to your children."

Alanna stared gloomily at the fire. "It doesn't matter, anyway. I prefer to be alone."

"No one prefers to be alone."

"I do." Alanna reached for the marshmallows she had placed on the table as Silas sat down on the other chair. "I don't do well with other people."

Silas tilted his head to the side. "What do you mean?"

"People start to dislike me once they get to know me."

"Are you sure it isn't the vibe you're putting off—that you don't want to be friends?"

She took a marshmallow out then picked out a long stick. "Matthew is mad at me, and I hurt Ginny's feelings."

"Why is Matthew mad at you?" Silas took the thin stick away from her to give her a thicker one.

"He scared me, and I told him to take his filthy hands off me." Alanna bit down on her bottom lip then grimaced when pain shot through.

"Yeah, I wouldn't do that. The swelling hasn't gone down." His gentle gaze made her start to tear up. "Why did you say that to him?"

"He grabbed me to keep me from falling off that cliff, but I didn't know that. He startled me."

"Hmm ... Did you tell him that?"

"I started to. Then I figured it might be better if he stayed mad at me. He's better off not having me as a friend."

"What happened with Ginny?"

"I asked her last name so I didn't have to use her first name. She wouldn't tell me, so I asked the sheriff."

"For the same reason? Because you make a terrible friend?"

Alanna leaned forward in her seat to put the marshmallow into the flames. "I like your family, you seem to be really nice people, but I shouldn't have taken the job."

"Why not?"

Alanna moved her gaze away from the flames. "I don't want any of you to be hurt. I couldn't live with myself if anything happened."

"Who would hurt us?"

"Two people who would have no hesitation of hurting anyone, not even Freddy, to get back at me."

"I see," he mused. "It's done."

"What is?" She stared at him blankly.

"Your marshmallow."

"Oh ..." She grinned. "It's a good thing I like them crispy." Alanna blew on it to cool it down.

"As far as Mathew is concerned, he'll get over his anger. He gets hot, but he cools down eventually. Ginny forgot her hurt feelings within seconds. It'll just make her more determined to become friends with you."

"I'm getting that vibe from her."

They both started laughing.

Alanna continued roasting marshmallows as Silas pulled the steaks off the grill then put more on.

"You must go through a ton of meat."

"There's a farm over the state line that I go to; buy from it in bulk. When I go, you can come with me, if you want."

"The sheriff won't let me go across the state line."

Silas shrugged. "Won't hurt to ask."

"No, it doesn't." Alanna looked at the charred crust on her marshmallow and inexplicably wanted to cry.

As if sensing her mood, Silas sat back down in his chair. "Alanna, the thing is, when you drag old baggage around with you, and you find something new, you don't have a place to put it."

Her shoulders slumped. "I've been carrying mine around so long that I wouldn't know how to let it go."

"That's easier than it seems. Just get rid of the old baggage and allow yourself to make room for new experiences."

"I don't want anyone hurt ..."

"You said Matthew and Ginny were already hurt by you not letting them in today. I tried to protect my brothers and sisters by leaving to get a helmet. While I was gone, my dad crashed with Leah on a four-wheeler. If I had been there, neither of them would have been riding without a helmet."

Alanna saw the deep regret on his face. "You can't hold yourself responsible—"

"No, I can't. I agree with you ... not any more than you

can hold yourself responsible for the actions of another person. You can only be responsible for the hurt you cause. You don't have to be afraid of those two people any longer. The Colemans are a tough breed. We've been surviving on this mountain for generations, against all the odds."

"You never had to deal with people like Owen and Kate before," she warned.

The look that came over Silas' face had her nearly dropping her marshmallow stick into the fire.

"They've never dealt with the Colemans."

Chapter Thirteen

Alanna was cutting another bite of her steak when three trucks pulled in.

"I thought you said they wouldn't be back until later?"

"They must have finished early. Don't worry; all the swelling has gone." Silas wasn't perturbed by her accusing tone.

Alanna blushed at Silas' astute gaze as his brothers piled out of the trucks, giving whoops of, "Hell yeah!"

Unable to hold back her smile at their boisterous behavior at sighting Silas at the grill, she held her plate tighter, now knowing why Silas had made so many steaks. They were fantastic! If she hadn't eaten so many marshmallows, she would have pulled a Greer and taken another one.

"They get excited anytime we grill out." Silas attempted to excuse their behavior when Jody nearly ran Ezra over to reach the steaks on the folding table first.

"Where are the plates?" Ezra frantically turned his head as he stood guard over the steaks.

"In the kitchen," Silas told him. "We didn't expect you back yet."

"Isaac, get the plates, forks, and knives!" Jody bellowed out, shoving Ezra aside.

Silas stood up. "Ezra, you and Jody get the lawn chairs while I dig the potatoes out." Silas gave her a wry glance when they took off toward the house without an argument. "We haven't grilled out in a while, so they're *really* excited."

"You don't grill often?" she asked.

"You kidding, right?" Fynn grinned at her, taking Silas' chair. "Do you know who our neighbor is?"

Alanna shook her head. "No. Why?"

"Greer Porter," Matthew supplied, his arms filled with cans of soda in one arm and a case of beer in the other.

Alanna choked on a bite of her steak.

Silas patted her on the back until she managed to clear her airway.

"How close?"

"Close enough I'm surprised he isn't here yet," Matthew said, taking a lawn chair and setting it between hers and Fynn's.

Silas handed Matthew and Fynn plates. "He's on duty."

Alanna loosened her grip on her plate.

Matthew's eyes dropped to her hands. "Greer really messed with you, didn't he?" Noticing Silas' questioning look, he explained, "Alanna told us how Greer drove her crazy when she was in jail."

Silas nodded. "He does have that effect on people."

"He's why you don't grill out often?" Alanna unwrapped her steaming potato.

"He has a nose that would put a bloodhound's to shame," Moses said, adding a steak to the plate Silas had given him. "Greer's a bottomless pit. He could eat all our steaks and still ask for more."

"Greer expends a lot of energy," Silas said.

"From searching for his next meal," Moses joked.

"I can't argue with that." Silas gave up defending Greer and changed the topic. "What happened about the fence? I didn't expect you for a couple more hours."

"Al twisted his ankle in the dark," Matthew said drily. "He's letting us come back in the morning."

Fynn noticed the marshmallows and candy bars. "Can I have a s'more?"

"After you finish your steak," Silas agreed.

Alanna sat quietly, enjoying listening to the group of men talk and tease each other. Feeling someone watching her, she realized Matthew was staring at her.

"How's the allergic reaction? Are you feeling better?" he asked softly, in an undertone, so as not to disturb the others talking.

"Much better, thank you." Setting her fork and knife on her plate, she said, "I feel bad I won't be able to help out milking the goats."

"Silas will take over doing it. None of us go near those four-legged mules after Moses's arm was broken by one of them."

"They're really sweet."

"That's easy for you to say. You're a woman."

"So I've been told," she joked.

Matthew's eyes held hers. "By whom?"

Her contentment vanished at the memory of when she had been brutally shown the difference between boys and girls.

"Um ... I don't remember." Tearing her gaze away, she started counting the potatoes pulled from the fire. There should be five left. Seeing Silas hadn't come back outside from going to get more candy bars, Alanna moved away from Matthew to grab the long, metal spoon Silas had used to scoop them out with. She was careful as she used the spoon to shift the ashes, unearthing a spot of foil. When she lifted the potato out, it slipped off the spoon. Not thinking, she went to catch it, and a hiss of pain escaped her when two of her fingers came in contact with the hot ashes.

Matthew shoved his hand into the flames to block her hand when she unwittingly jerked her hand upward toward the flames instead of keeping it low to slip underneath, as Silas had done.

Holding her hand to her chest, she tried to take Matthew's to see how badly he had been burnt.

"The flames didn't get me. Let me see your hand." He inexplicably held his hand out to her. It didn't have a mark on it.

She gingerly extended hers, and Matthew cupped the bottom in his.

"What happened?"

Alanna blinked back tears when Silas walked up next to them.

"I was getting another potato. Before you say anything, I know you told me not to."

"I wasn't going to say anything." Silas' gentle gaze had her putting on a brave face in front of him, while Matthew's searching gaze wasn't buying her calm.

"Jody has some first-aid supplies at his trailer. I'll walk her home and put some cream on for her." Removing his hand from under hers, Matthew cupped her elbow. "Let's go."

"I can find the supplies. You don't have to leave."

"I was getting ready to leave, anyway. I have to be up at six in the morning to be at Al's."

"Here, Alanna." Fynn held out a s'more he had just made, wrapping it in a paper towel. "I'll make me another one."

Alanna started to refuse, but didn't want to hurt the little boy's feelings. "Thank you."

She didn't resist Matthew's tug on her arm, wanting to be

back in the trailer alone so she could finally have the cry she had held back earlier.

Matthew brought them to a stop at his workshop. "Wait here. I want to get a flashlight."

He carried his cell phone as a flashlight when he disappeared inside the building and came out a minute later.

"Doing okay?" he asked.

"Uh-huh ..."

He turned on the flashlight, and they continued on to the trailer without talking. Alanna was thankful he wasn't making small talk; she didn't think she could hold it together if she showed one crack in her control.

Inside the trailer, Matthew ordered her to sit at the small kitchen table before disappearing into the half-bathroom. He came back out with a small plastic box. He opened it and took out some gauze, burn cream, and Tylenol. Then he moved to the refrigerator and took out a bottle of water. Removing the cap, he set the water down in front of her. Then, opening the Tylenol, he handed her two.

"Take them. They'll help with the pain."

While she took the pain medication, Matthew carefully grabbed her wrist so he could raise her hand. Alanna looked away at seeing the pad of four fingers and the side of her thumb had blisters forming.

"Hold your hands still." Matthew went to the sink to wash his hands before placing a towel onto the table. Alanna was surprised his gentle, calloused hands were able to touch her without causing pain.

Alanna lifted her eyes when he finished wrapping her fingers in gauze.

"Make sure you don't get it wet."

"I won't." She felt embarrassed. He was being so nice to her. She didn't know if she could turn the other cheek as graciously as he was. "I'm sorry for snapping at you earlier today."

"You've already apologized."

"You didn't look as if you believed me."

"I did." Matthew put the items he'd used back in the box then closed it with a snap. Softly placing a finger on one of her gauzed fingers, he said, "It wasn't the flames that damaged your hand; it was the smoldering ash." He raised his unburnt hand that had blocked hers from getting hurt further. "I've worked with fire my whole life. I should have been more careful how I touched you. My skin is thicker than it seems."

"Are you comparing me to fire?"

Matthew gave her a sexy smile that rocked her world. She was glad she was sitting down.

As he tucked a loose tendril of her hair behind her ear, he let the knuckles of his hand trail down her cheek before letting his hand drop to his side. "You should come by the shop tomorrow afternoon. I'll show you some of the work I do."

Matthew carried the box back to the bathroom. When he returned, he asked, "You good for the night?"

"Yes." Alanna started to take a bite of the s'more, but Matthew beat her to it. Then, giving her a wink, he started for the front door.

"Hey! That was mine."

"You snooze, you lose around here. Besides, I saw that marshmallow bag when we got home. It was half-empty. I just saved you a stomachache. Come lock the door after me."

After she locked the door, Alanna went to the bathroom to shower off the thick smell of smoke from her body which wasn't easy with one hand. Once she was done, she slid on a pair of pajamas.

In bed, she turned off the bedside lamp. The tears she had been holding back were gone. Matthew's kindness and the talk she'd had with Silas about carrying old baggage made her realize she had spent so much of her life in fear of Owen and Kate and didn't remember one moment of joy that hadn't been marked by them.

She had lost her childhood to their depravity, her foster mother, who had tried to be a buffer between them, her relationship with her foster brother, Sam. She had stopped dating one guy because she hadn't been able to loosen her guard enough to be intimate with him ... She had missed out on so much. In hindsight, she had made so many mistakes. She would do it all over if given the chance.

Rolling over, she promised herself that she was done with the baggage. If there was something that made her unhappy in the future, it would be discarded.

Closing her eyes, she drifted off to sleep, not worried about nightmare figures chasing after her in the dark. Her dreams were of her sitting by the bright glow of the firepit, with Matthew sitting next to her.

Chapter Fourteen

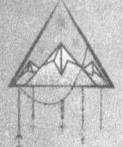

Matthew used the towel he had hanging across the back of his neck to wipe the sweat away from his face. Partially closing the billow, he lowered the flames as he turned the metal rod in them.

"I'm beat."

Matthew spared a brief glance at Isaac, who was laying a completed iron spike on a worktable.

"Go ahead and go. I'm almost finished with this one."

"You sure?" Isaac asked, using his own towel to wipe the sweat running down his chest.

"I'm sure. I've got it. This finishes the order—"

A knock at the door had them both turning their heads. Usually, everyone just walked inside.

"Come in," Isaac called out.

Matthew held his breath, hoping it was who he thought it was. And when Alanna walked inside, the tight restriction in his chest eased.

"I was beginning to think you wouldn't come." Turning back to the iron spoke, he put the tube that controlled the blower in his mouth to continue twirling the end of the spoke in the flames in series of quick jerks with one leather-gloved hand, while using a sculpting tool to make the indentions he wanted in the iron.

"You can sit here." Matthew heard Isaac showing her where to sit. "I was just leaving," he told her. "Matthew won't be long. He's just finishing the last one we need to get done."

"I can come back later. I don't want to disturb his work."

"You're good. We're used to having someone around. Fynn just left. He got a one hundred on his science exam, so he wanted to show it off. There are drinks in the cooler next you. Help yourself."

Out of the corner of his eye, Matthew saw Isaac give a quick nod to Alanna before he left as she took one out. He forced his eyes back to the spoke instead of watching Alanna rub the cold bottle of water across her forehead.

"I should have expected it to be hot in here," she said, curiously watching his movements.

Shutting off the blower, he took the spoke out of the fire. It was a piece of shit. He had lost his concentration the moment she had walked inside the building.

"We can go outside. I need to cool this down."

She was on his heels as he moved toward the door.

"How do you work in this heat?" She waved her hand to fan herself.

Taking a pair of long-handled tongs, Matthew submersed the spoke in cold water that was in a barrel to the side of the workshop.

"I like the heat." He shrugged, watching a drop of sweat roll down her neck to slide between her breasts. She looked as pretty as a picture today. Something was different about her, but he couldn't pinpoint what it was.

"How's your hand?"

"Blistered, but at least it doesn't hurt. I wanted to babysit Freddy today, but Moses beat me to it."

"You're not supposed to start until Monday," he reminded her, seeing the disappointment in her eyes.

"Are you sure it wasn't because I seem to be accident prone around you guys?"

"You really can't say an allergic reaction is an accident. You were unaware of your reaction, or you wouldn't have gone near the goats."

Alanna narrowed her eyes on him. "Ginny showed you the picture she took of me, didn't she?"

Matthew pulled the spoke out of the water then laid it on the worktable set outside the window of the shop. "I refuse to answer on the grounds it will incriminate Ginny," he teased.

"Anyway ..." Alanna deliberately changed the subject with a moue of self-disgust at herself. "I'm really not accident prone. The goats were a fluke, and my burnt hand was the result of my gluttony."

"Be careful. Gluttony is one of the seven deadly sins."

"Really? Then I hope Deputy Porter is a churchgoing man."

"Poor Greer," Matthew mocked. "I wonder if he is aware of the affect he had on you."

Alanna rolled her eyes at him. "Don't you dare tell him. He already thinks I was trying to tempt him into breaking his marriage vows."

"You're joking?"

"I really wish I were. He told me he barely had enough stamina to satisfy his wife."

"Greer always did think he was a ladies' man."

"Are we talking about the same man?"

"He didn't appeal to you?"

"Noooo." Alanna made an aghast face.

Matthew picked up the iron spoke. "What type of man are you attracted to?"

"I don't have a particular type."

Matthew tsked her. "Yes, you do." Matthew started walking away. "Come on; let's go back inside. It should have cooled off by now."

It was still hot, but more bearable, as he had damped the fire before leaving the shop.

Laying the iron spoke on the worktable, he took off his remaining glove.

He turned and saw her standing by the iron door he had made, leaning against the wall. Striding quickly to stand next to her, Matthew prepared to pull her away if she so much as tried to lift a finger to touch it, regardless if she snapped at him or not.

"Careful. The door is heavy."

He expected her to give him a wary look at how close he was standing next to her, but she seemed unconcerned, keeping her gaze on the intricately carved door.

"You do beautiful work."

"Thank you."

"You and Isaac made this?"

"Yes. We have a catalog of ironwork we can produce."

"Do you only work with iron?"

"No, it depends on what the customers want."

Matthew showed her around the shop, the different metal they worked with, then some of the finished products, which were stored there, waiting to be installed.

"Jody and Jacob normally install and deliver our products, while Isaac and I work here."

"That's cool that you get to work with your brothers. You all seem to get along very well."

"We have our moments. Moses prefers to work alone, which is why he trains dogs."

"And Ezra?"

"He builds furniture. Sometimes, he works with Silas."

"Managing your mountain?"

Matthew raised an eyebrow at her. "Silas didn't tell you what he does for a living?"

"No."

"Silas likes to enter competitions, or he used to. Lately, we've been keeping him busy helping us out. He's the one who taught Ezra woodworking, so if Ezra gets a big order, he'll pitch in to get the order out. They just completed a large bedroom set."

"I envy your family's talents. I don't have a talented bone in my body."

"What are your interests?"

"I'm afraid I don't have any. I'm the most boring person you'll ever meet."

"What do you do in your free time? Watch television, read books, play video games?"

"No. I hadn't read a book in years until I went to jail. That's all there was to do there."

"So, what do you do in your free time? I don't believe you just sit and watch the walls."

"No. I usually don't have a lot of free time. When I'm not working, I babysit for a couple of mothers in my neighborhood who work the evening shifts, and when I'm not doing that, I online tutor children who are behind math and reading."

"Children are your interest."

"I guess. It isn't much to brag about, though."

"I bet it is to the mothers you help out. If you like working with children, why didn't you become a teacher?"

"I have a degree in Education, but I moved to Ohio and wasn't licensed there. I had already racked up enough in loans, and I didn't want to add more to it by taking more classes to get licensed in Ohio. In case you didn't know, teaching isn't a very lucrative career. Real estate pays much better."

"Does it make you feel as good?"

"No, it doesn't." She shrugged. "Unfortunately, my bills need to be paid. Eventually, I'll go back and get the classes I need when I pay my loans down some more."

"Sounds like a good plan."

Checking that the fire was out and the two side windows were closed, Matthew went to the cooler to grab a drink.

"What are your plans for the rest of the day?"

Alanna raised her hand with a wry twist of her lips. "Nothing. Silas and Ginny refuse to let me do anything until Monday."

"Then I have a suggestion."

"What?"

"Depends," he teased, reaching for his shirt on a peg on the wall.

"On what?"

"Are you allergic to fish?"

Chapter Fifteen

"Can you put another worm on the hook for me?"

"You're losing a lot of worms and have no fish to show for it." Matthew gave her a broad grin when she showed him the empty hook.

Alanna shot him a harassed look. "The fish are against me."

Matthew reached into the plastic cup beside him to pull out another fat worm. Scooting over on the blanket he had brought, he took her fishing pole to put the worm on the hook.

"You're good to go," he said, handing the pole back. Remaining seated where he was, Matthew laughed at her grossed-out expression. "It doesn't hurt them."

"Who told you that? I bet it wasn't a worm."

Matthew laughed. "My dad, and I'd bet his told him the same thing."

"There has to be a more humane way to fish."

"There is, but fresh bait is always best. I could look for some crickets when we run out of worms."

Alanna gave him a withering stare. "I meant something that doesn't involve killing another living creature."

Matthew cocked his head sideways. "You do know I plan to clean and fry the fish we catch, right?"

"I'll worry about that when we catch one."

"Ye of little faith," he mocked.

"Pretty sure you saying that is sacrilegious," she chastised.

Matthew released a low whistle of appreciation. "Look at you sounding like a Kentucky girl. Next thing I know, you'll be sneaking off to go to church with Greer."

Alanna lowered her eyes to half-mast. "Do you have a death wish?" she asked sweetly.

He raised a cocky eyebrow at her. "Who would you get to kill me? You can't stand to hurt a worm."

"You mention Deputy Porter again, I'll make an exception."

"Good luck with that. I plan to live forever."

"No one lives forever."

"I might not live forever, but I do plan to live long enough to break the record of being the oldest person to ever live."

Alanna's eyebrows climbed. "How old is the current record holder?"

"One hundred and twenty-two years and a hundred and sixty-four days."

Her eyebrows climbed higher. "You want to live to be over one hundred and twenty-two years?"

"Don't you?"

Alanna looked toward where her bobber was floating in the water. "I've never thought about it. My parents both died young. I've never pictured myself as an old woman."

"You think you're going to die young?"

Matthew saw her slightly nod.

"You're not," he said confidently. "You're going to live

forever, like me. I'm going to share the secret to longevity with you."

Alanna turned to smile at him from over her shoulder. "Tell me, oh wise one," she mocked.

Studying her, Matthew saw the deep sadness in her eyes. He had to grip his fishing pole to keep from pulling her protectively into his arms. Instead, he looked around, pretending he was afraid of listening ears, then lowered his voice. "Love," he whispered as if it were a state secret.

"*Love?*" she scoffed at him. "How does that make you live longer?"

"Because your memory never dies in the ones you leave behind. With all my brothers, Ginny, and all the children I plan to have, I will live into infinity."

Alanna lay back on the blanket, setting her fishing pole next to her. "How many children do you plan to have?"

"I plan to outdo my dad. I'm going to have ten children."

"Do all your family members want large families?"

"Yes, that's why we work so hard, so we won't have to sell any land off. We want to have our own little town."

"That makes sense; you all had a happy childhood and want to share the same experience with your own children." Alanna curled onto her side, laying her cheek on her arm.

Matthew rested his weight on his elbow to stare down at her. "How many children do you plan to have?" Matthew saw her lashes fan across her cheek when she closed her eyes.

"None." She opened her eyes. "I can't have children."

Matthew felt as if someone had just snuck up behind him and stabbed him in the back.

"You can't or won't?" he asked hoarsely.

"Can't."

He wanted to ask her why, but knew it wasn't the appropriate question to ask. He had been focused on his pain and had missed the grief in her eyes. Slowly, Matthew reached down to trail a lone fingertip over her exposed cheek.

"I'm sorry. You love children, so that must be hard for you."

"I don't let myself think about it often."

"Then we'll change the subject. Luckily for you, I had a feeling we wouldn't be having a fish fry, so I brought some sandwiches."

Her expression lightened. "So, we can stop fishing?"

"I take it you don't like fishing?"

"It won't be on my list to try again, no," she said, straightening back into a seated position.

Matthew tugged the nylon bag he had brought from his home. He opened the bag and took out the two sandwiches he had prepared, handing her one.

Her eyes widened when her hand dipped at the weight. "I can't eat the whole thing. This is enough to feed three people."

"Or"—he grinned, opening his own mammoth-sized sandwich—"you and the person sitting next to you."

"Now that makes sense."

"Yes, it does. Just eat as much as you like, and I'll finish it off."

"What if I ate most of it?" she teased before taking a large bite of the sandwich.

He delved his hand back into the bag, pulling out three bags of chips, bottled waters, and four candy bars.

"You're a man who thinks of everything," she complimented.

"I try to. I wanted you to enjoy yourself."

"Why?"

Matthew used the pad of his thumb to wipe the dollop of mustard away from the corner of her mouth. Bringing the thumb to his mouth, he licked it off. "A man who wants to live forever would be lonely without a fishing buddy by his side."

Alanna blinked at him. Matthew could see she wasn't ready to believe what he ached to tell her.

"But I hate fishing."

"We could do other things than fishing," he suggested.

Matthew saw her throat move under her fair skin.

"Like what?"

"I can teach you how to play with fire."

Chapter Sixteen

God, help me. She had never wanted to fan her heated face more in her life. Sitting next to Matthew after seeing him shirtless at his shop was a trial in endurance. Wanting to take the towel and wipe the sweat away from his chest ...

When she had walked inside and saw both shirtless men, she had no difficulty keeping her eyes off Isaac while Matthew's bare chest had drawn her gaze like a magnet.

Both men were handsome, had almost similar hair color. Matthew wore his closely cropped, while Isaac's dark-brown was much longer and tied back. Matthew was taller than Isaac, while Isaac was stockier.

Women in her real estate office would be using their manicured nails to scratch each other's eyes out if they came in to buy a house. Hell, they would probably hand their own home over.

The main difference between them was the way Matthew made her feel. She had never been attracted to a man the way she was to him. That was the main problem with her—she had never been truly attracted to a man before. When she had dated a single father after moving to Ohio, she hadn't moved past a few dates when it became plain she could not reciprocate his burgeoning feelings for her, and couldn't give him the smallest intimacy, such as a small kiss, without recoiling.

Far from recoiling, she wanted to wind herself around Matthew's body until he would need pliers to peel her off him.

Realizing she had been staring at him like a lovesick teenager, she raised her bandaged hand. "I tried playing with fire and got burned."

"You can't live your life afraid of pain. I hear childbirth involves a lot of pain. Women still have children. I burned myself numerous times when I started working with fire. The shop I have now is the third one. The other two burnt down. You learn to minimize the pain and move on. That's why women have more than one kid, and I built my last shop of out of metal."

"I love how you compare losing your shop to childbirth. If men gave birth, humankind would cease to exist."

"I can't argue about that. Dad made us boys watch a video of a woman giving birth." Matthew hung his head. "I think it emotionally scarred Jody," he whispered, as if sharing a family secret.

Alanna tore another bite off her sandwich then handed the rest to him. "I must have seen the same film." She laughed "Made me feel better about not having any."

Matthew's smile vanished.

She laid her bandaged hand down on his. "It's okay. I learned to deal with the knowledge since I was thirteen."

"That's a young age to find out something like that."

Alanna looked over at the small pond that Matthew had told her was created by run-off from a mountain stream.

"Could have been worse." She shrugged. "I could have not known then been blindsided when I was ready to start a family." Turning her eyes back to face him, Alanna caught the tormented expression on his face. "Hey, it's okay. I shouldn't have told you. I don't know why I did. I've never told anyone, not even my foster mother."

Matthew rewrapped what was left of his sandwich. "Alanna ..."

"I made you lose your appetite." She couldn't explain why she suddenly felt teary-eyed, as if she had stolen something precious from him. Alanna shook her head to clear her thoughts. "We were having fun. I didn't mean to spoil the good time we were enjoying."

"You couldn't spoil a second of time I get to spend with you."

Flushing, she removed her hand from covering his. "Did Silas tell you that Ginny won't get to her shopping tomorrow?" Alanna didn't give him time to answer. "I won't be needing you to go to my home to get my things. What Mrs. Bates gave me is more than enough to get me through. I asked one of the women I work with at the real estate company to pack up my personal belongings and put them in storage, and sell the rest, including my house."

"Silas told me. So, you're selling your house?"

"Yes, I only moved to Ohio because I was getting away from a bad situation. When my court case is over, I'll either be in prison or I can go wherever I want to live."

"Might as well plan to live here. Kentucky is going to steal your heart."

She had a terrible feeling a part of Kentucky already had. Each time she looked into Matthew's eyes, she felt as if he was stealing another part of her soul.

"It wouldn't be hard to do. I've only been here three days, and I feel more at home than I ever felt in Ohio and Indiana."

"Must be me." He grinned.

Alanna laughed at his shameless flirting. "No, it's the fishing." Alanna picked up her fishing pole as if it was the most important thing in the world that she caught a fish.

"You suck at fishing."

She lifted her eyebrows at him. "Excuse me? Where are the whoppers you caught? I'm not the only one fishless."

"Fishless?"

She shrugged. "You know what I mean."

"The fish aren't biting because the water is cold. The fish are going to the bottom of the pond, where it's warmer."

"Then, why have we been wasting our time?"

"I couldn't think of another way to get you to go on a picnic date with me."

Alanna met his eyes. "This is a date?"

"Yes, for Kentucky, it's a normal first date."

"Really?"

"Well"—he grinned—"it is when your date has to wear an ankle monitor."

Alanna embarrassedly looked away from him. He had only been joking with her, like he did with the rest of his family. During the two dinners she had spent with him and his family, he had been constantly joking with them.

Matthew tugged on a lock of her hair, making her return her eyes to him. "I even took a picture of our first date."

She wasn't going to fall for his joking a second time. Reaching for a plastic baggie of marshmallows, she popped one into her mouth with a disbelieving look.

"I did," he insisted.

"Show me," she called him out.

"All right." Matthew picked up his cell phone. Swiping his finger across the screen, he turned the phone to show her.

She burst out laughing. He must have taken a picture of her when she had tried to put her first worm on. She had thought he was putting his on, too. Instead, he had taken a picture of her.

"That's not fair. Delete it."

"Heck no. When we're fishing buddies at the ripe old age of one hundred, I can show you this picture and remind you that your fishing hasn't gotten any better."

"That's cruel."

"No crueler than the torture you inflicted on that poor worm."

"I pretended it was Greer," she shamefully confessed.

"You're bloodthirsty, woman." His grin widened. "I like it."

Alanna giggled then wanted to smack herself for sounding like a teenager. Embarrassed, she reached for another marshmallow, only for Matthew to take it out of her hand.

"You're driving me nuts by eating it plain. I brought graham crackers and chocolate bars for you to make some s'mores."

"We don't have a fire."

"You don't have a problem eating cold marshmallows, but you don't do cold s'mores?"

"I was saving the calories."

"You were being lazy."

"I was." She nodded.

"Then I'll make you one."

"Go ahead."

Alanna watched him assemble the s'more, waiting for him to hand it to her when it was done.

"You have a bite on your line."

She jerked her eyes toward her bobber as she used her uninjured hand to grab her fishing pole. She watched the bobber; it didn't move. Alanna turned back to Matthew.

"Did it get away? It isn't moving."

"Probably took the bait and fled."

"Little asshole," she fumed, setting the pole back down.

"Here you go," Matthew said, holding the s'more out.

Alanna took the s'more, feeling warmth from the cracker. She raised it to eye level and realized the chocolate was melted, and so was the marshmallow. It even had a crusty edge.

"How did you do that?" she asked, lifting wondering eyes to his.

"Magic."

Chapter Seventeen

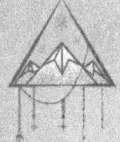

"Come on; how did you do it?"

His eyes twinkled with laughter when he opened his hand to show her the lighter.

Alanna moved to sit cross-legged on the blanket. "I love s'mores," she said, taking a bite.

"Especially when you don't have to make them," he teased her.

"Aren't you going to make you one?"

"You could give me a bite of yours."

Alanna started to break the s'more in half, like she had the sandwich, but Matthew grabbed her wrist and pulled it toward his mouth. Her body melted into a warm vat of honey when he opened his mouth and took a bite from where she had. When he released her hand so she could take it back, she lost all brain function when the tip of his tongue came out to lick a spot of chocolate from the corner of his mouth.

From the look in his mischievous eyes, Matthew was well aware of what he was doing. How could he not? A man who looked like him would have to be buried under a rock, on planet Neptune, for women not to lust after him.

Not thinking, she finished off her s'more as Matthew placed everything back in the cooler.

"Tomorrow, Silas is going to take a short drive across to West Virginia to buy some more meat to restock our freezer. You want to come with us?" he offered.

"I would love to, but"—Alanna straightened her legs and gave a wave toward the ankle monitor—"as you can see, I can't go."

"Don't worry; I'm sure Silas can convince the sheriff to let you go."

She gave him a doubtful glance. "I doubt it. The guidelines I have to follow are pretty straight forward. If I take one step off the range I'm limited to, I go back to jail."

"Do you want to go or not?"

"Yes, I would love to."

"Then leave it to me and Silas."

"Okay ..." she drawled out. "But if I have to go back to jail, you better bring me a s'more with a nail file in the middle."

"I won't have to do that. I'll just bribe Greer with a sixteen-ounce porterhouse to let you escape."

Her mouth dropped open, and she smacked her forehead at her stupidity. "Why didn't I think of that?"

Matthew tapped his fingers on his temple. "When you're dealing with Greer, you have to think on his wavelength."

"Food." She nodded, refraining from hitting herself again.

"Food." Matthew grinned. "And when that fails, there's one other thing he can't resist."

"Baked potatoes?"

He laughingly shook his head. "Money."

"Really?"

"Oh yes. Greer loves money as much as he loves food."

"I still can't believe he's married. His wife must be a saint."

"Holly watches over Greer like a hawk. She's afraid he'll get busted for selling his pot around town."

"Does the sheriff know?"

Matthew gave her a *are you kidding* look. "Knox is Greer's best customer. The whole town knows Greer and his brothers grow the best pot in Kentucky. To be truthful, the best in the country."

"You're joking?"

"Nope. Pot business in Kentucky is no joking matter. We can walk around the property, if you want, and I can show you the no trespassing signs marking where their property begins. Anyone takes a step on their property, they know about it, and they don't need dogs to alert them. The Porters have set booby traps everywhere to keep people out of their crop."

"How do they get away with that?"

Matthew arched a brow at her. "Did you miss where I said the sheriff is Greer's best customer?"

Matthew rose from the blanket to hold out his hand. "You want to go for that walk?"

"Oh yes, I've got to see the signs. What do they do with the trespassers? Call the sheriff?"

"No, everyone knows if you take a step on their property, you're taking your life into your own hands. There's a reason Greer is deputy, even though he's a pain in the ass. He's one of the best shots in the county."

"*One* of the best?"

Matthew didn't release her hand as they took off walking. "His brothers, Tate and Dustin, and his sister, Rachel, have a running competition on who's shot more kills."

Alanna stopped walking at his choice of words. "Kills? Animals?"

"People."

She stared at him, dumbstruck, and then used her shoulder to bump him. "There's no way. You're pulling my leg."

He tugged her hand to get her moving again. "Okay. I'm joking."

Alanna stared at his profile. He did seem to be serious, but she wasn't having the wool pulled over her eyes again. Her lips twitched. He was really reaching this time. She would be shocked if Greer could get his gun out of the holster. He would be too busy eating to be bothered.

When they came to the first sign, Alanna burst out in laughter so hard she had to hold her stomach. "*Move the fuck on or get shot!*"

"That one's pretty tame."

"Does your family post signs to get back at them?"

"Of course."

Walking a little farther, they came to another sign.

Alanna had to hug the wooden fence post when she read it to keep from doubling over. "*This steer isn't for you, Greer. Move along.*' Oh my God, this is priceless. Does it work?"

Matthew gave her another *are you kidding* look. "What do you think?"

"Are there more?"

"Oh yes. Greer loves making signs. He changes them out every couple of weeks."

Matthew walked her around their property, showing her the different parts where the Colemans' land intersected with the Porters'. "We think this could be in the direction of where he grows his plants."

She didn't have to step forward to read the sign; she could read it from where she was standing. "'Monitored by ...'" she read out loud. Underneath the words was a picture of a rifle instead of a camera. Then there was another one posted right next to it. "*You're sixty seconds from meeting the undertaker.*'" Alanna looked around, not seeing any from the Colemans. "You let him have these?"

Matthew pointed up, and Alanna looked to where he was pointing.

There was a target on the same tree that the Porters had posted sign. In the middle of the target was a picture of a hand giving the *fuck off* sign. She stared at the sign appreciatively.

"Do you know how many times I wanted to do that when Greer was driving me nuts?"

"I'm guessing a lot."

"Are his brothers like him?"

"Yes, and no. Pretty much no one messes with Tate. No one wants to get on his bad side, while everyone likes Dustin. He's become a financial advisor. I hear he's pretty good at it."

"How about his sister?"

"Rachel married a Last Rider. She works for them, too. Every so often, when she's searching for a certain plant, she comes here to ask Silas for permission to search for it on our land. Rachel is a botanist. She has a doctorate in aquaculture. Three times a year, she takes samples from our streams, pond, and our well water."

"Has she found anything interesting yet?"

"If she has, she hasn't told us yet. Remember, at heart, she is a Porter; if she found anything really good, she'd be afraid we wouldn't let her come back." Matthew looked up at the darkening sky. "We should head back. I didn't bring a flashlight with me. I'll walk you to the trailer then grab a flashlight from Jody's to go back to the pond to get the poles."

Alanna hated for the day to come to an end. She had enjoyed spending most of the day with him. Even before she had found herself in jail in Treepoint, her days had been plodding along with boring regularity. Even the happiness she found babysitting or tutoring was short lived, as if there was a storm cloud just waiting to break and send catastrophe showering down. She hadn't felt like that today. The whole day had been spent with the sun shining down and no cloud in sight.

Matthew waited at the bottom step when they reached the trailer.

"Other than the fishing, I had fun today. Thank you."

Matthew put his hand over his heart. "I'm crushed that you didn't like fishing. Next time, I'll teach you how to shoot a bow and arrow so you can be my hunting buddy if fishing isn't your thing."

Alanna gave him a baleful look. "What have you got against animals?"

"Nothing. I love animals, especially when they're large enough to have four points on their antlers, and I can get a couple of roasts out of them and several pounds of stew meat."

"Are you a better fisherman or hunter?"

"The same."

Alanna opened the door to go inside, but couldn't resist a parting shot.

"Then I think the animals are safe."

Chapter Eighteen

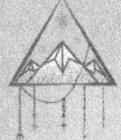

Matthew walked back to the pond without bothering to get the flashlight. He could easily see in the dark. The only reason he had gotten the flashlight the night before was so Alanna could see where she was walking.

Slinging the nylon cooler strap onto his shoulder, he gathered the poles, blanket, and tackle box then walked to his house, where he dumped everything on his front porch before he started walking toward Silas' house. Each step he took, the mix of emotions he had been holding all afternoon assailed him in wave after wave of grief.

As he neared Silas' porch, he had to bend over to place his hands on his thighs to catch his breath. His whole body was shaking with raw fury and anguish so deep that he felt the burning sting of tears in his eyes. Righting himself, he went around the corner to walk up the steps of the porch.

He slowed when he saw all of his brothers and Ginny were there, waiting for him.

Reaching the porch, he went to the banister to grip it tightly next to where Ezra was sitting on top.

After two deep breaths, he was able to manage to turn his head to stare at Ezra. "You knew."

Ezra's eyes were filled with pain yet stoic. "Yes."

Turning around, Matthew pinned his eyes on Fynn, who was standing next to Silas, who had a protective arm around their younger brother. "You saw."

Fynn only nodded.

Matthew took a step forward, unable to prevent himself from reaching for Fynn.

"Matthew, he's only a boy."

Matthew pulled himself out from under Silas' hold to pull Fynn close. Giving Fynn a hug, he had to clear his throat before releasing him and turning him toward the door. "Go inside."

The boy didn't move.

"I want to stay," Fynn argued.

"Go inside, Fynn," Silas ordered.

Reluctantly, his little brother went inside.

Matthew waited until the door was closed to ask the question that had been pounding through his head all day.

"Why can't she have children?"

Silas went to sit on the banister next to Ezra. "Owen."

"I'm going to kill him," Matthew vowed, taking a step toward the end of the porch.

Isaac, Moses, Jacob, and Jody blocked him.

"You can't," Ezra warned, remaining seated where he was.

Matthew clenched his hands into fists by his sides as he glared at his brothers blocking him. "Did you know?"

They all shook their head.

"Silas only told us a couple of hours ago," Isaac said.

Around the same time Alanna told me, Matthew surmised.

Matthew spun around to glare at Silas accusingly. "But you knew all along, didn't you?"

"Yes, I found out when she came out of the doctor's office

when her case manager took her when her foster mother became worried after Alanna didn't start having her periods." Silas' face was stone cold as he talked, yet his eyes shared the grief Matthew was feeling.

Silas paused, knowing how the next words would affect him. "She was thirteen."

"That's when you said she quit talking to you."

Silas nodded. "She grew depressed, quit eating, and all she wanted to do was talk to me and you, whether she was inside or out. The medicine they put her on muted my voice, regardless of how hard I tried."

"Why in the fuck did you tell me I would have ten children, Ezra?" he shouted at his brother.

"You will have ten children—five boys and five girls. They just won't come from your body."

"You left that last detail out."

"I had to." Ezra sighed. "If I or Silas had told you before, you would have killed Owen, and Alanna would have never come to Treepoint. I can't change the way the stars are written. I wish I could." Ezra's expression became resigned. "There was no way they would have let you have ten children. We're too powerful. Generations have grown on this mountain." Ezra nodded at all his brothers. "Yet, there are eight of us. Other than the Porters, we don't have any kin spread out in the county or living in other states. We all want big families. If each of us has at least four children, and they have four children ... they will always limit our numbers to protect us."

"I wanted too many, so they are giving me none?" he said achingly, wanting to rage against the gods, but knowing if he did, the reprisal would be swift in coming.

Ginny moved away from the banister she was leaning against. "They are giving you ten children," she said softly with tears in her eyes. "Ten children who won't grow up fatherless or motherless." Walking toward him, she took his clenched fists in her hands. "Ten children who you can give the same wonderful childhood you had, that we all had. Did you feel any differently toward me when I told you that I wasn't your biological sister?"

"No!" He loved Ginny just as much as he had loved Leah.

Matthew stared down at Ginny's swollen belly. He was never going to see Alanna swell with their child. It had been stolen from them, just like so many other firsts had been stolen.

Matthew broke, unable to hold back, his face cracking. "I wanted to be the first one to hold my own son when he was born."

Ginny released his hands to hug him close. "You won't be holding a son you created, but you will hold your son. It's doesn't mean it won't be just as meaningful."

Isaac moved up next to him, placing his arms around him and Ginny. "You can hold my son first," he offered.

Matthew felt Jody's and Jacob's arms surround them.

"Mine, too," Jody said.

"Same, bro," Jacob added.

Moses's hand landed heavily on his shoulder. "Ezra won't tell me how many I'm having, but, dude, you've got first dibs."

Matthew heard the slam of the screen door.

"You can have mine. I don't want kids." Fynn sidled under his brothers to wrap his hands around Mathew's waist.

Matthew lifted his eyes to where Ezra and Silas were still sitting, seeing the same thing in their eyes that he had always seen when they talked about his future with Alanna. Never-ending love.

"At least tell me you didn't lie about how old we'll live to."

Ezra gave him a stank face. "Bro, I don't know why you want to live so long. You'll have to have prosthetic balls."

Matthew felt love surrounding him and knew he didn't have anything to complain about. He was already blessed with his family, his soul mate had finally found her way to him, and she seemed to be starting to like him. Having his own children would have just been the cherry on an already heavily decorated cake.

"That's easy to answer," Matthew scoffed back. "At least one of us has to outlive Greer."

Chapter Nineteen

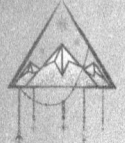

"I'm not going." Alanna took another look at who was sitting in the front seat with Silas and started walking back to her trailer.

"Come on, Alanna."

Alanna heard Matthew hurrying to catch up with her.

"I promise he will behave. This is the only way the sheriff will let you go."

"Then I won't go."

"Come on," he wheedled. "He won't say a word, I promise. They have fresh apple cider and caramel apples."

He had her at the apple cider.

Spinning on her tennis shoes, she gave him a threatening glare. "If he so much as touches my caramel apple, I will shove it down his throat," she warned.

Matthew raised a hand, as if pledging. "I'll do it for you."

Alanna poked a finger in his chest. "I'm going to hold you to that promise."

Matthew nodded solemnly.

They walked back to Silas' truck, and Matthew held the back door open for her behind Greer, allowing her to slide inside. Alanna stared straight ahead as Matthew closed the door and went to the other door.

"Let's hit the road," Matthew said enthusiastically, closing the door once he was inside.

"About time."

Greer's sarcastic voice sounded like nails on a chalkboard to her.

Matthew gave her an apologetic glace as Silas pulled out of the driveway.

"Mind turning the radio on, Silas?"

Quiet music filled the cab of the truck as Silas pulled onto the main road in the opposite direction of Treepoint.

As Silas drove, everyone was silent, including Greer. Alanna was able to relax back in her seat and look out at the scenery. The trees were beautiful as they started getting their springtime buds. Staring at them, she began to realize she wasn't seeing the tree trunks; she was gazing at the top of the trees. Leaning her head closer to the window, she glanced down to see the huge drop-off. They were climbing the mountain and going higher.

"Are you afraid of heights?"

Alanna turned away from the window to smile at Matthew. "No. One of the few things I'm not afraid of."

"See if you can say that in about ten minutes. We're going to be coming down, and then going up that big mother." Greer pointed toward the front windshield.

Alanna tilted her head sideways to look around Greer's seat. She stared ahead.

"I thought you said you weren't afraid of heights," he teased.

"I'm not. I'm just stunned at how pretty it is."

The hour-long drive wasn't as bad as she had expected it to be. What had been unexpected was her queasy stomach from the curvy mountain road. At one point, she thought she was going to vomit.

"Silas, you might need to pull over," she gasped out, putting a hand over her mouth.

Greer turned around to give her a handful of strange-looking candy. "Suck on one of these."

She glanced down at her bandaged hand, holding the candy suspiciously. "What are they?"

"Homemade ginger candy." Greer frowned. "What do you think they are?"

"I don't know."

"Oh ..." Greer turned back around.

Matthew gave her a laughing look. He knew what she had been suspicious of it being.

Opening one of the hard candies, she put it in her mouth. After a few minutes, her stomach quit rolling with each curve of the road.

"None of your brothers or Ginny wanted to join us?" she asked to take her mind off the twists and turns.

"No." Matthew gave her a sympathetic glance. "Ginny's stomach couldn't handle the turns any better than you, and all the boys went out hunting this morning."

"They better not be hunting on Porter land. They'll get their asses shot off," Greer snarled from over his shoulder.

"They won't have to," Matthew assured him. "All the deer are on Coleman property."

Alanna was relieved when Silas took a turn-off marked with *"Sunlight Farm and Orchard."* There were several cars parked when they arrived.

Getting out of the truck, Alanna could hear the squeals of children's voices.

"Save me," Greer groused. "I couldn't get away from kids for a day to save my life."

Greer walked alongside Silas, while Matthew and her walked behind them.

Greer gave her a cautionary glare. "Make sure you stay within my sight. You aren't going to escape on my watch."

Alanna couldn't take it anymore. She raised her hand to—

Matthew caught her hand. "It's not worth it."

"Not to you, but it would be to me."

"Be the bigger person."

"Okay."

She decided to pretend Greer wasn't there and not let him ruin her day.

"Where are we heading first?" Matthew called out to Silas.

"The barn. I need to place an order."

"They don't have goats, do they?" she whispered aside to Matthew.

"No. They have cows, lambs, and pigs."

"Do you think I could be allergic to them?"

"Just don't touch any of them, and you should be good."

The barn was a pretty good walk. They had to pass the apple orchard and what seemed like a produce stand attached to a building where people were coming in and out, carrying bags.

"It's a longer walk than I expected."

Matthew nodded. "To keep the customers from smelling the animals.

Her nose told her when they were getting near before she spotted the big red barn.

As they walked inside, a stocky man, who was talking to another, excused himself to greet Silas.

"Hey, Silas. Haven't seen you around in a while. I was beginning to think you went vegan."

"Jimbo." Silas took the hand held out to him. "Brought some company with me today. You know Greer and my brother, and this is a friend of ours, Alanna."

"Nice to meet you." Alanna took the hand extended to her, quickly pulling back after a second. The man might be friendly, but she recognized a familiar meanness in his eyes.

Shivering, she edged closer to Matthew, who wrapped his arm around her waist and gave a brief glance in her direction.

The friendly façade began to fade when Jimbo's ruddy face turned in Greer's direction. "I thought I told you not to come here anymore."

"He's here with me," Silas interjected smoothly. "I'm paying for his order today."

Alanna looked at Matthew. Now she understood how Silas had gained permission to leave the Colemans' property.

"In that case, let's get your orders written up." He pulled up what looked like a handheld computer dangling from his jeans. "I have several you can look over. I have a real beauty over here."

Jimbo started walking to a stall that had a metal gate, and they all followed him

"I hoped she would be a prize-winning milking cow. She's been dry as a bone, so I've been fattening her up."

Alanna instinctively stepped forward, unable to resist the big soulful eyes.

"Aw ... She's so sweet." She reached out to touch the nose that was trying to get through the gate.

"Nuh-uh. Let's not chance it," Matthew warned, pulling her hand away.

"I'll take her," Greer spoke up right away.

Jimbo pressed the keys on a machine.

"How do want the meat parceled out?"

"Parceled out?" Alanna whispered, horrorstricken.

"Give me out forty percent in a variety of roasts, ground me up around thirty percent—the youngins like their hamburgers — and the rest in steaks."

Alanna reached into her pocket for another piece of ginger candy.

"I'll get as many out of her as I can." Jimbo let the machine go to hang back as his side and nodded at another stall, one over. "Now, this one over here is a little smaller, but she's grass fed."

Alanna didn't move away with the men, feeling the cow staring at her pleadingly.

"What's wrong?" Matthew asked, coming back.

"They're going to kill her," she said starkly.

"Yeah, that's why we came here—to replace the meat we ate."

Her hand went to her stomach. "She looks so sweet."

Matthew looked at the cow. She could tell he wasn't as taken with her as she was.

"Is Alanna okay?" Silas asked, coming back.

"Alanna doesn't want the cow killed." Matthew gave Silas a helpless glance.

"Too bad. She's gonna be on my dinner table," Greer said unsympathetically. "Going to feed us for at least six months."

"You'll make it last three months," Matthew retorted.

"Don't matter. It'll be three months of pure pleasure I don't have to pay for." Greer grinned.

Alanna lost it. She sprung forward, her feet leaving the ground, her eyes on his throat.

Matthew caught her mid-leap with an arm around her waist.

"Matthew, why don't you take Alanna to the store?" Silas placed himself between her and Greer. "Stock us up on what we need. Ginny's wanting two bushels of apples."

"She ain't supposed to be out of my sight," Greer snapped, starting after them as Matthew tried to usher her away.

"Then you can go with them. I'll pick the hog out for you," Silas said benignly.

Greer stopped in his tracks. "You going to buy me some pork?"

"Depends." Silas arched a brow at him.

"You kids go on." Greer turned back to Silas, pulling his jeans up higher. "We have some business to take care of."

Alanna barely made it out of earshot. "I can't stand that man. He's going to kill that sweet cow."

"If Greer hadn't picked the cow, someone else would have. Probably Silas. Greer wouldn't kill it himself ... Well, he would if ..."

"I don't mean Greer. I mean Jimbo," she hissed out his name.

"Yeah ... he's the one who kills them. But to be fair, that's what he does for a living ... and you didn't have a problem eating that ribeye on your plate the other night."

"I'm never going to eat another meat product," she vowed then remembered how good the steak tasted. "At least, not after I meet them. How can you raise an animal to slaughter? Wouldn't you get attached?"

Matthew started to look uncomfortable.

Alanna narrowed her eyes on him. "You have, haven't you?" she asked him accusingly.

His cheeks were becoming flushed. "We don't get attached to farm animals," he tried to explain. "We don't pet them or give them names."

Alanna jerked her hand free. "What have you killed?"

"Not much. A couple of chickens ..."

"What else?"

"Nothing ... But Isaac or Silas do kill goats for—"

Alanna raised her hand to prevent him from saying any more. "They kill goats?"

"*They* did ... I didn't," he assured her.

Alanna thought of those sweet goats chomping on twigs.

She had enjoyed working with them until she turned into the Bride of Frankenstein.

"Will you tell them not to do it while I'm there?"

Matthew eagerly nodded. "Of course."

Alanna relaxed her rigid posture. It wasn't like his brothers were slayers of cute animals—chickens weren't cute. Still, she didn't want them killed.

"At least there's one good thing."

"What is it?" she was forced to ask when he playfully bumped her shoulder with his.

"At least you never met any of the goats or chickens in the freezer."

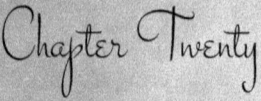

Chapter Twenty

Entering the store, Alanna was charmed by the old-fashioned atmosphere of wooden barrels filled with their homemade products, baskets of apples, and jars and jars of preserved fruit, jams, and vegetables.

The store was bustling with customers while a woman behind a wooden counter checked them out.

"Hello," she greeted them when they entered through the door. "If you need anything, just yell out."

Alanna didn't know where to start. She wanted it all.

Matthew must have picked up on her hesitation. Under his amused gaze, he led her to the shelves.

"This is as good a start as any. See anything you want?"

She saw several. The problem was she didn't have any money.

"Pick out anything you want. Silas will pay for it. It'll go in the storeroom, so if anyone wants it, they can take it. That includes you. Just make sure to buy several enough to last for a long time. We only come here a few times a year."

She couldn't resist the peach preserves. She took one jar.

Matthew took five.

"I love peach cobbler," he explained at her surprised look. "I'm going to set these on the counter and grab a basket. I'll be right back."

Alanna let him take the jar she was holding.

She was deciding on whether to get the cherry or apple pie filling when she saw a frail woman coming out from a back room. Alanna smiled at her when the woman noticed her gaze on her. She was wearing the same green-colored smock the woman behind the counter was wearing. At her smile, the woman came out from the back room and made her way toward her. She must have misunderstood her smile as needing help.

Each step the woman took, she would have to lift up the long metal cane attached to her arm. Glancing down, Alanna could see one of her legs was shorter than the other and she was wearing a thicker sole shoe on that foot. Alanna felt bad that she was wasting a trip to see if she needed anything, so she walked to meet her.

"I don't need anything," she said, turning her head to see where Matthew had gone. Turning back, she saw the woman staring at her quizzically. "I'm fine. I don't need anything," Alanna repeated.

The woman's face cleared with an understanding smile.

"Hey, Hanna Joy." Matthew came to her side, holding a basket in his hand. He set the basket down and began making a series of hand movements as he talked. "*How have you been doing? I didn't see you the last time I came with Silas.*"

The woman leaned the cane on her hip as she started signing back. "*I stayed with Livia while I had another surgery on my hip.*"

Matthew spoke the words out loud as Hanna Joy signed, and then he signed back.

"The surgery must have gone well. I thought you were

going to break a speed limit for a second." His teasing had the woman laughing.

At her laughter, Alanna realized she was much younger than the initial impression she had given. Alanna had thought her to be over thirty. With laughter relaxing her face, Alanna thought she might be in her mid-twenties. The way she wore her brown hair coiled back, no makeup, made her look older, and the drab smock wasn't helping either. Alanna thought the jailhouse orange had done her no favors, but that puke green was atrocious.

"*The surgery went longer than expected, but I can walk with one cane now.*"

Alanna was listening to the signed conversation between Matthew and Hanna Joy when the bell over the door rang. Jimbo, Greer, and Silas walked inside, spotting them.

"So I see ..." Matthew was signing when Jimbo reached them first.

"What are you doing out of the house?" he yelled, lowering his face to Hanna Joy's, who shrank back when he moved to place himself between her and Matthew. "I told you I would take over for Livia."

Alanna started to give the overbearing farmer a taste of his own medicine at speaking that way to the cowering woman. From Silas' , Matthew's, and Greer's expressions, she wouldn't be the only one.

"Stop it, Dad."

The other woman came from behind the counter to take Hanna Joy by the shoulders, moving her aside. From the sharp movements she made as she talked, Alanna guessed she was shouting in sign language.

"She was here for a minute to give me a bathroom break because you were late getting here."

"I was busy," he snarled.

"Which is why I suggested for you to hire extra help, which you refused."

"I don't need extra help. I have Dean. He'll be back tomorrow."

"Dean quit!"

"He'll be back; you'll see!"

"Okay ..." the woman drawled out, rolling her eyes at her father before turning her gaze to the rest of them watching the interaction. "Sorry for the commotion," she apologized.

Alanna wanted to tell her it wasn't her place to apologize for the way Jimbo reacted.

"No need to apologize. I'm afraid we're who kept Jimbo busy," Silas said with a quiet voice, signing as he talked.

Something in his tone had Alanna looking at Silas' face. Alanna smiled at the woman when Silas caught her staring at him, introducing Livia.

"It's nice to meet you," the woman greeted her with a smile before turning a fuming smile back to her father. "Since you're here, I'll take Hanna Joy back to the house and make lunch."

"It's nice seeing you, Livia," Silas said, reaching into a barrel next to him, which held tiny bottles of honey. "How long are you staying?"

"I was supposed to go tonight, but I'm going to wait and see if Dean shows up tomorrow," Livia explained.

"Might as well go. I don't need you," Jimbo barked.

Alanna noticed that, while both Silas and Livia signed so Hanna Joy knew the conversation going on around her, Jimbo didn't.

Livia disdainfully ignored her father. "Nice to see you again, Silas, Greer, Matthew. Alanna, it was nice to meet you."

"You find anything you want?" Matthew asked as the two women left the store and Jimbo stomped toward the counter, where customers were lined up, waiting.

"I was trying to choose between cherry and apple pie filling," she told him.

"We can get them both." Matthew took several jars of each type to place in the basket he was holding. Alanna didn't miss the way Silas watched the women walk past the window until they were out of sight.

"When you going to ask her out?" Alanna heard Greer ask behind her back.

"I have," Silas said. "She told me no."

"Then move on. You ain't getting any younger."

"Shut up, Greer, and pick out what you want."

"You don't have to tell me twice," Greer said, happily getting a basket.

Silas stayed with them as they picked and chose several more jars from the shelves.

Watching him, Alanna saw the dejected expression he was attempting to shield by asking her if she had ever tried chow chow.

"No, I haven't. What does it taste like?"

"Similar to relish."

"That makes sense since that's what it looks like."

They browsed around the store until Greer caught up with them.

"You see the jugs of apple cider?" he asked. "I got two for me and one for the youngins."

"We got six," Silas told him, lifting them to place them on the counter. "And Jimbo is getting another three. Each of the boys will get their own jug, Ginny, and Alanna."

"He has more out back?" Greer asked eagerly. "Might as well get a couple more to freeze for me."

It took Jimbo three more trips to the back room before Silas was ready to check out.

"Anything else, Silas?"

"Each of us will take one of those caramel apples, and you can bag seven more for us to take home."

Alanna took one of the apples Jimbo held out for them. The caramel melted in her mouth, and the apple snapped under her teeth, which she nearly spat out in surprise when Jimbo told Silas how much he owed.

"You okay?" Matthew asked when her hand went to her throat.

"Did Silas buy the whole orchard?"

"No." Matthew stared at her in amusement. "He bought three cows, two pigs, two—" He stopped at seeing her aghast expression. "Never mind. You're better off not knowing."

"You think?" Greer quipped, taking a big bite of his apple.

"Alanna, you and Greer can go on back to the truck while Matthew and I load up the dollies. We shouldn't be long."

She wasn't crazy about being left alone with Greer, afraid he would say something that would send her over the edge and find herself back in jail.

Thankfully, Greer was too busy eating his apple to talk.

Climbing into the back seat of the truck, she started to close the door.

"Don't bother. I want to take a gander of that hand of yours."

"It's fine." She attempted to close the door again.

"I'll just open it again," he warned, opening the door to the front seat.

Alanna lifted her head to see what he was doing. Greer was taking out a first-aid kit from under the seat.

He put the stick from the candy apple in the trash Silas had hanging from the glovebox, then moved back to where she was sitting.

"Scoot over."

Alanna scooted over on the seat, watching as Greer climbed inside to set the red box on the seat between them.

Opening the box, he took out a small bottle of hand sanitizer and squeezed some on his hands. When he was done, he held out his hand. "Now let me see."

"I told you it's fine." Holding her apple, she tucked her bandaged hand in the crock of her other arm.

"I told Knox I would make sure you're healing okay. If you won't let me, I can take you to the emergency room and get them to do it for him."

She held her bandaged hand out for him to unwind the gauze.

"It looks much worse than it is. The blisters popped ..."

Greer stared at her hand. "It's getting infected. Are you running a fever?"

"N—"

She wasn't finished answering when she felt Greer's hand land on her forehead.

"What are you doing?" she said, pulling her head away.

"Checking for fever. Eat your apple. I have some work to do."

Alanna resumed eating her apple as Greer held her burned hand and started sifting through different creams in the box.

"You don't have to hold my hand while you're opening the bottles," she told him, watching him try to open the creams one-handedly. "I'm not going to escape."

"I didn't reckon you would," he said, finally getting the cap off. "You don't like me much, do you?"

Alanna looked from her hand to meet his eyes. "Not really."

Greer grinned at her. "Can't say I blame you. Most people don't. It's no never mind to me whether they do or don't." He shrugged.

Alanna saw Greer truly couldn't care less what people thought of him, and a grudging respect for the man started to bloom in her chest. She wished she could have that attitude without the obnoxiousness.

"Why?"

"Because, at the end the day, I only have to settle up with one person, and you, nor any of them, are that person."

"You're right."

"I always am. No one can make you feel less than you're worth unless you let them, and I don't let 'em."

"You might not, but for others, it's not so easy."

"It's just as easy as you want it to be, or just as hard. All you need to do is remember two little words."

"What are they?"

"Fuck 'em."

Her lips twitched in laughter. Those two words did sum up Greer's attitude.

"I take it you don't care about those no trespassing signs the Colemans posted to get back at yours."

"Course not." He snorted. "Those are for kiddies; mine make them think twice."

"Yes, they do." Alanna couldn't hold back her gurgle of laughter.

"There you go. You'll be right as rain tomorrow," he said, snapping the case closed.

Alanna stared at her newly bandaged hand. She must have zoned out while they were talking because she didn't remember him reaching for the gauze.

"There comes the boy, right on time. One of those jugs of apple cider is riding home on my lap." Holding on to the door, Greer started to jump down from the seat to the gravel parking lot.

"Greer!" Alanna scooted over the seat when she saw he would have fallen if he hadn't been holding the door.

Silas and Matthew came running up.

"You okay, Greer?"

"Yes. Just came down the wrong way," he said, limping to the passenger door. "Here, help me up in the seat, Matthew."

Matthew lifted Greer into the front seat.

"Hand me one of those jugs of cider," Greer demanded before Matthew could shut the door.

Silas handed him one, giving him a suspicious glance and shutting the door before Greer could ask for anything else.

Alanna leaned forward. "Are you sure you're okay, Greer?"

"Yep," he said, taking a drink from the gallon-sized jug.

Looking out the window, she saw Silas and Matthew unloading the two dollies.

"I didn't know they had bags of flour."

"Ain't flour; it's cornmeal. Those bags weigh a ton to lift."

Alanna poked her head around to see Greer unconcernedly drinking his cider while watching the other men unload the cornmeal and bushels of apples and potatoes.

"I know what you're thinking," he said, seeing she was watching him.

She narrowed her gaze on him accusingly, feeling all the goodwill she had started to feel from bandaging her hand go up in smoke. Greer was deliberately not helping them. "I bet you do."

He narrowed his back at her. "Then I guess you know what I'm saying back."

Chapter Twenty-One

Alanna blinked to clear her blurry gaze. Yawning, she opened the freezer in the storage building to take out a package of frozen sausage before moving to the other freezer to take out pre-made waffles. After making sure she marked the items off the inventory list, she gathered them to leave the storage building.

She turned on her flashlight and started walking toward Silas' home. The eerie silence in the morning was giving her second thoughts about being out so early. She was dreading walking back through the wooded area of the property she had to cross to reach Silas' home. On her way to the storage building, she could have sworn she had felt eyes on her the entire way.

Her hand trembled on the flashlight as the eeriness enveloped her again. Then she froze in place when she heard a small sound. Raising the flashlight upward, she narrowed her eyes. Was a rabid squirrel about to attack her?

At a small movement between the branches of a tree, Alanna started screaming, afraid she was about to be pounced on by a fox, a racoon—

"Alanna, stop screaming," Matthew's frantic whisper had her pausing mid-scream.

"Matthew?" she angrily yelled, shining the flashlight higher. "What are you—"

"Shh ..." he whispered.

With an open mouth, she watched Matthew climb out of some crazy chair attached to the trunk of the tree. She snapped her mouth closed when he climbed down the tree until he was standing next to her.

"What are you doing out so early?" he asked.

"I wanted to have breakfast ready for Fynn before he went to school. It's his birthday."

"I know. I wished you had told us."

Alanna shined the flashlight on what was hanging from his shoulder. "What is that?"

"Nothing ..." Matthew took her arm to propel her to start walking again.

"Is that a bow?" Alanna stopped moving. "Are you out here hunting?" She jerked the flashlight up to shine it on his face.

Matthew took it away from her.

"You are! What are you hunting?"

"I wasn't hunting ..."

She pursed her lips at the deceptive ring in his voice.

"I was just watching Fynn trying to get his first buck."

"Fynn's here?" Alanna started shining the flashlight through the trees.

"Oh my God ... get her out of here!" Isaac hissed from overhead.

"Well, that's not very polite!"

Matthew started propelling her through the woods. "Isaac gets a little irritated when he's tired."

"How long have you guys been out here?"

"For a couple of hours."

"I should go back and get another roll of sausage. I can make breakfast for everyone since they're all up."

"Let's not." Matthew hastened their steps so they were moving through the wooded section fast.

When they reached Silas' house, she started for the kitchen to get cooking as Matthew placed his bow next to the door and quickly followed on her heel.

"About breakfast..."

Alanna turned with the sausage and waffles in her arms.

"Silas and all of us go to Waffle House to celebrate birthday mornings."

"That would have been nice to know."

Matthew glanced down at her ankle monitor. "We would have told you, but we didn't want you to feel bad when we couldn't invite you."

"That's okay." Alanna went to the freezer and placed the sausage and the waffles inside.

"How about you go ahead and cook? I'm sure Fynn—"

"My breakfast is no comparison to Waffle House," Alanna cut him off, smiling to show him that she wasn't offended. "I don't want to spoil Fynn's birthday tradition." Covering her mouth, she started to yawn, debating on getting started on Silas' chores or returning to her trailer.

"Why don't you take a nap?"

"I was thinking the same thing. I was just deciding whether to go back to the trailer or do the chores and sleep later."

Matthew frowned. "Why not just take a nap here instead of going back and forth?"

"I couldn't do that."

"I don't know why not," he said firmly, taking her hand and leading her down a hallway to a door that was always closed when she was here. Matthew opened it then stepped aside to watch her reaction.

"Is the bed really hanging from the ceiling?"

He grinned. "Yes. Dad made it for Ginny and Leah to lie on so they could watch the stars at night." The room was surrounded with curtained windows.

"You miss her very much, don't you?" Alanna tightened her hold on his hand at the painfully sad look in his eyes.

"There isn't a day that goes by that I don't think of her. She was a beautiful child who had the most loving heart of any person I ever met. Until you."

Blushing at the way he looked at her, she embarrassedly lowered her gaze to take in the outfit he was wearing. Not even ugly green camouflage could make him look bad. In fact, the tight green T-shirt emphasized his muscular chest.

Becoming aware that Matthew was giving her a knowing grin, she hastily tried to turn the heated atmosphere down a few degrees by giving him a threatening glare.

"Were you out there trying to kill Bambi's mom?"

"*Me*?" Matthew put a hand to his chest in innocence. "No, I was watching my brothers trying to bag Bambi's dad."

"That's just mean."

"That's just life." He casually closed the door to lean back against it.

Alanna raised an eyebrow at his obvious ploy to keep them closed off if any of his brothers came.

"You have to take a few out so the population can remain healthy and thriving," he explained.

"If you weren't planning on shooting one, why did you take your bow?"

"Protection."

She couldn't help but giggle at his unrepentant smile. "How are you always in such a good mood?"

Matthew stepped away from the door to move closer to her. "Why wouldn't I be?" he said seriously. "I have every-thing I could ever want on this mountain. The only thing that was missing was having a woman of mine to share it with."

Alanna took a step back. There was no way she should be feeling the scope of emotions Matthew brought out in her so quickly.

"You want to go swinging?"

Before she could answer, she found herself falling back onto the bed, sending it swinging. Turning her head to yell at him for being sneaky, she felt it die in her throat at the laughter in his eyes.

"Have you ever heard the country song "Swingin'"?

"No, I can't say I have."

Matthew lay down next to her, sending the bed swinging again. "It's an oldie but goodie."

He started singing with an old-fashioned twang, which had her curling up in laughter.

"I used to come downstairs when Ginny and Leah were lying here and sing it to them then start swinging the bed. It drove them crazy."

She winced. "I can sympathize. A singer, you're not."

Matthew rolled to his side to face her. "You don't think so? I'm crushed."

"Does nothing get you down for long?"

He braced his head on his hand. "No. Why should it? Life is too short not to make the most of every minute, and I refuse to give sadness more than five minutes of my valuable time." He traced the line of her nose, and when he reached to the tip, he branched out to cup her cheek then slide down to place his palm over her heart.

How could he seduce her with one hand? Not to mention the warmth from that one hand extended to her whole body.

"I don't think living to be over one hundred constitutes as being short."

"No amount of time with you is ever going to be enough."

"You might not be a good singer, but you would make a great songwriter."

Matthew arched a brow at her.

"You don't believe me?" She stared into his eyes, only to fall further under his spell. Unable to help herself, she raised her head and did something she had never done before. She kissed Matthew.

She felt his hand go behind her neck to keep her from pulling back as he parted his lips. When he didn't take over the way she had expected him to, she grew bolder, letting the tip of her tongue slide into his mouth. The kiss turned into a bonfire.

He scooted closer to her, his chest practically covering hers as she explored his mouth. She felt herself melt when his hand went to the curve of her hips, tugging her closer until their bodies were melded together as their kisses grew wilder.

Desperately wanting to get even closer, she slipped her hands under his shirt, and then she lost what little sanity she had left at the feel of his skin under her hands. She felt as if she was lightning in a bottle, raw power contained in a living, breathing body. At any second, she felt like she would lose whatever control she had and the bottle would break.

Alanna couldn't think of any instance in her life where she had actually been daring. Kissing Matthew was the most daring thing she had ever done. It was too late to second-guess if she should. Way too late. She was becoming afraid, that like the metal he worked with little effort, Matthew could bend her to his will.

She became so lost when his hand went between her thighs to rub her cleft before unbuttoning her jeans to lower the zipper. She twisted her hips under his hand when he started playing with her clit. As his fingers moved faster, she felt a sudden unbelievable emotion she had never felt before. Sensations rippled through her, making it impossible to deny what had just happened.

Breaking the kiss, she sat up with a jerk, gasping for breath. He didn't try to pull her back down. Instead, he removed his hand to rub her back in long stokes, easing the desire that had spiraled to a flame out of her control.

Embarrassed, she practically lunged off the bed, forgetting it was elevated. She would have taken a nosedive if Matthew hadn't caught her and slung her back onto the bed.

As she stared up at the ceiling, she blew a swath of hair out of her face to see Matthew's contagious grin smiling down at her.

"This is so embarrassing."

"Why?" he asked, tucking her hair behind her ear.

"I'm supposed to be working, not playing around."

His grin slipped. "I wasn't playing. Were you?"

"Matthew ..."

He pressed a firm finger on the lines of her frown.

"Nuh-uh ... I'm not going to let you ruin it."

She refused to meet his eyes. "Ruin what?"

He clicked his tongue at her. "There you go again. Don't worry." He placed a chaste kiss on her forehead before getting off the bed. "I won't rub it in that I just gave you the best orgasm known to womankind."

She gaped at how loud his voice was, never mind the bragging tone he used, which had her holding back from laughing.

"Shh ... Someone could come in."

Matthew gave her a wink. "Okay, we'll just keep this on the down-low."

Alanna could only shake her head. "Go away."

"Is that any way to speak to the man who just gave you—"

Rising up in one movement, she snatched up a pillow and threw it at him.

Matthew ran for the door, his laughter trailing after him.

"Goon," she snorted out, watching as he grabbed his bow before taking off out the front door.

She jumped out of bed and started to run after him then realized there was a side door just inches away. Rushing to open the door, she gave Matthew a smart-alecky smirk.

"You better not kill Bambi's dad!" she screeched as loudly as she could. Seeing the pained expression on his face, she rubbed her hands together as if she had just finished doing a great job, then shut the door.

"That'll show him."

Her glee vanished in a second when she realized she had slammed the door open with her jeans still unzipped, showing her belly. Burning embarrassment had her lifting her hands to her burning cheeks. She zipped her jeans back up and smoothed her T-shirt back down.

"The best orgasm known to womankind." She sniffed inelegantly then started grinning.

Damn. He wasn't wrong.

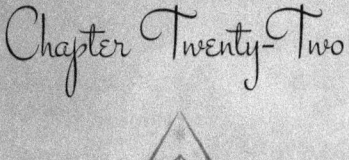

Chapter Twenty-Two

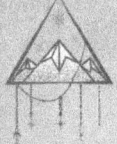

Alanna tickled the baby as he held his favorite stuffed lion protectively clutched to his chest.

"Got you." She picked the baby up, sending him into peals of laughter.

"I see you two are having fun," Ginny said as she walked across the room.

"You have a good nap?" Alanna placed Freddy back on the floor, returning the lion to him.

"Yes. Thank you. You two eat lunch?"

"Yes, and Freddy finished his whole bottle. Can I do anything else for you before I leave?"

"No, I'm good. Where are you off to now?"

"Silas wants me to meet him at the storage building. We're going to organize the new stuff we brought yesterday."

"I missed going this year," she said regretfully. "But I did enjoy the apple and cider Silas brought us last night."

"You're lucky Silas caught Greer trying to slip another one out of the bag."

"Greer was just messing with Silas. He knows Silas would

drive back to replace it. He won't bring us anything unless there's enough to go around."

"Silas is a good person."

"The best," Ginny agreed.

Alanna paused before moving toward the door. "Can I ask you ...? Never mind. I'll see you tomorrow."

Ginny looked at her curiously. "What were you going to ask?"

"I shouldn't."

"Go ahead ... My sister has been too busy to come over for a chat lately. I need some girl talk."

Alanna frowned. "I thought your sister was dead?"

"One is. I'm adopted."

Alanna had to sit down when Ginny started explaining how she had ended up being adopted by Freddy Coleman.

"I can't believe I didn't recognize you." Alanna sat in stunned amazement that she hadn't recognized the singer she used to listen to regularly.

"I wasn't that popular, and I haven't played in public in quite a while."

"Just make sure you tell me when you do. I would love to hear you sing in person."

"I will." Ginny smiled. "So, what question were you going to ask me?"

"After I went to your other home to do what they needed done, I realized Matthew hadn't shown me his place. When I went to his shop, he said he didn't need anything done. Is there a reason he doesn't want me to do anything?"

Ginny stared down at her feet. "I don't believe so. He's probably just being a slob, and he's waiting until he has time to get it clean before letting you inside."

"Oh ... You think he's embarrassed?"

"Definitely." Bending down, Ginny lifted Freddy into her arms.

Alanna could have sworn she heard a smothered giggle coming from Ginny, but when she looked up, she wasn't laughing.

Leaving, she was relieved Matthew wasn't against using her to do chores around his house, like Moses was. She could understand Moses not wanting her around his place because of the dogs he was training. She had seen him occasionally around the property, trailing after the dogs, expecting them to follow him, yet he was the one following from behind. When he had introduced her to the dogs, he had her stand still and told each of the six dogs to sniff her. After that, he had left with them.

All of Silas' brothers had been friendly to her, with Matthew being the friendliest, and Moses and Isaac being the most closed off. Fynn and Ezra, she had been around the least. Matthew had told her during their walk yesterday that Fynn and Ezra were close and spent a lot of time together. Judging from cleaning Jody and Jacob's trailer, those men were fixated on their video games and food, reminding her that she needed to pick up several items they wanted restocked.

Silas' truck was just pulling up the road leading to the outbuilding as she came down the rise from Ginny's home. She came to a stop then started running when she saw there was a trailer attached to his truck and she could see what was inside.

She ran up to Silas' truck as both he and Matthew were getting out.

"You bought the cow!"

Matthew leaned across the hood, grinning.

"Are you happy?"

"Ecstatic!" She made herself tone down her enthusiasm. "Thank you, Silas."

Silas shook his head. "Don't thank me. Matthew bought her for you."

She turned wondering eyes to him. "You did?"

"I did." He smiled, his eyes twinkling at her. "She's all yours. You're going to be the one to take care of her once we have you tested to find out if you're allergic or not."

"You'll have to show me how."

"There's going to be a lot of dirty work involved," he warned.

"I don't care." She went around the side of the trailer to see the cow from the opening.

"See? I didn't leave you." Alanna twirled around in joy, thrilled that the cow hadn't been killed. Then she turned to face Matthew, trying not to cry.

"I've never had such a wonderful present. Thank you."

"You're very welcome." Matthew walked to where she was standing. "You know what this means?"

She stopped smiling, fear gripping her heart so hard that she was afraid it had stopped beating.

"You'll have to stay in Kentucky. It's going to be hard to find a place in Ohio where you can keep a cow this size in your backyard."

She started smiling again. "I don't think she would fit in a rental car either."

"Nope, she won't," Silas said from the back of the trailer. Matthew and she walked to the back as Silas pulled the metal ramp down so he and Matthew could nudge the cow out of the trailer.

Both men were sweating when Silas closed the trailer.

"For now, let's put her in the old goat pen. I need to go the tractor store to get some hay." Silas used the sleeve of his shirt to wipe his brow. "Matthew, you mind helping Alanna organize the storage room?"

"Can do," he said from over his shoulder as he went to open the old wooden gate and Silas herded the cow inside the pen.

Running to where Ginny had shown her where the water hose was kept, she turned the spigot on, holding the hose where the metal met the rubber tubing, the way Ginny had shown her to because the connection was old and needed to be replaced. Carrying the hose, she ran back, waiting for one of the men to show her where to put the water. Her cow was probably thirsty after the ride across two mountains.

"There's an extra trough in the equipment building," Silas told Matthew, seeing her waiting with the hose.

"I'll get it," Alanna offered as Matthew started to open the gate so he could get out of the pen.

"It will be too heavy—"

Shoving the water hose at Matthew, she forgot to hold the connection until he took it from her hand. Matthew automatically reached out to take the nozzle, and when he did, water blasted him in the face.

"Oh my God." Alanna tried to grab the hose again, but Matthew had crimped it closed with his hand as he stared at her accusingly.

"You did that deliberately."

"I di—" She gurgled with laughter at seeing water drip off the tip of his nose. "Did not."

Matthew turned the hose in her direction.

"Don't!" she screeched.

Water hit her in the mouth.

She put up her hands up to protect her face, but the water was immediately shut off.

"Sorry, I didn't think about your hand getting wet," Matthew apologized.

"There's some gauze in the first-aid kit in the storage building," Silas said, closing the gate to look at their soaked clothes. "I'm going to head out while I'm still the only one dry."

Seeing the mischievous glint in Matthew's eyes at Silas'

bragging, Alanna blocked Matthew from showering Silas. "Don't you dare."

"You're no fun. It wouldn't hurt him to get a little wet."

"I don't think there was anything little about what you were planning."

"Come on; let's get that wet bandage off." Taking her by the wrist, he went to turn the water off before heading to the storage building. He released her wrist and turned on the light. It took the two of them searching to find the first-aid kit shoved on a top shelf.

"Just how many first-aid kits does your family have?" Alanna asked, taking a seat on a stool that Matthew showed her.

"A bunch. With all our homes spread out, Silas likes to be prepared in case of emergency." Matthew opened the first-aid box before unwinding the soaked gauze covering her hand. They both stared down at her hand. There wasn't a burn mark. Her skin was unblemished.

"Wow, you healed fast." Closing the box, he wadded up the gauze and threw it into the trash can by the freezer.

Alanna twirled her fingers, not even seeing the thin skin peeling where the blisters had popped.

Frowning down at her hand, she couldn't understand how it had healed so fast when it had been infected yesterday. Maybe the cream in the first-aid box was stronger than the cream she had been using.

"I bet I know how my hand healed so fast." Alanna looked up from her hand, catching Matthew's worried expression.

"How?"

"Greer must have used some of that oil they can get from pot." She nodded knowledgeably.

Matthew frowned. "What kind?"

"You know, that hemp oil."

His eyes started twinkling with laughter. "I think you mean CBD oil?"

"Whatever." She waved her hand, showing it didn't matter. "I wish he hadn't. What if the sheriff wants a drug test?"

"Why would the sheriff want a drug test?"

"I don't know. Don't they drug test all felons?"

"I guess, when they've been arrested on drug charges. You were arrested for kidnapping."

"Oh ..." She stood, considering what he had said, then came to a conclusion. "You might be right, but if I do get a surprise drug test, Greer is going down with me."

"You're on a first name basis with him?"

When had she stopped thinking of him as Deputy Porter? The simple thought shook her enough that she had to sit back down as Matthew shrugged out of his wet shirt to sling it down on the freezer. Bending down, he lifted a bushel of potatoes and placed it in a dark corner.

"Can I ask you something?" she asked as he bent down to pick up another bushel of potatoes.

"Shoot."

"Are you flirting with me because you know I will be leaving town when my court case is over?"

Matthew set the bushel back down with an angry frown. "What made you ask that?"

Alanna ran a hand through her damp hair, not meeting his eyes. "Silas said you get most of your orders from customers away from here."

"So?"

"You could be flirting with me and every other girl in or out of town. You say you're waiting for your soul mate; that could be your pickup line for all I know 'cause it worked on me."

She dropped her eyes when she saw the hurt in his eyes,

and then a blazing anger that had her jumping off the stool to back away from him.

"Don't you dare try to run from me ... ever."

She froze in place at the threat in his voice.

"No matter how angry I get ..." Matthew strode angrily toward her.

It was everything she could do not to run screaming at the top of her lungs. His friendly visage had been replaced with an extremely masculine one that had her trembling.

Reaching her, he wrapped his hand around the back of her neck. "I bought a fucking cow for you."

"I know," she said miserably.

"Shut up," he ordered before continuing stonily. "Which serves no purpose on God's sweet earth other than to eat and shit. There is no woman I would spend that kind of money on other than you. Ask me why, Alanna."

"No." She tried to shake her head, but his firm hand wouldn't let her.

His face became stonier. "*Ask me.*"

She closed her eyes tightly, terrified, wanting to block the question out of her mind.

"I already know," she barely whispered.

"Then tell me."

"Because you think I'm your soul mate."

Chapter Twenty-Three

"B ut you don't."

She closed her eyes again, unable to maintain eye contact with him. "I've lost my perspective. I need to stay detached and not care about anyone. Especially you."

"Why especially me?" The depths of his eyes searched her for a truth which was hard for her to admit.

"Because I don't even know if I have a future to share with anyone until my court case is over. Besides, I don't know what I'm feeling is ..." She cut herself off and changed directions. "You're a very physically attractive man who's paying attention to me. It's not like men are banging my door down. I like your family. I've always wanted to be part of a large family. You want ten children; did you forget telling me that? I can't even give you one." She gave one excuse after another to not have to explain how he was becoming the air she breathed.

"You're innocent of the charges that have been brought about you. Diamond will prove that fact. The only reason men aren't banging your door down is because men want a woman to light a fire in their balls, not freeze them off. I'm glad you like my family. I'd be more worried if you didn't. My family and I are a package deal." His furious expression began to lighten.

She was learning Matthew didn't have it in him to be angry long. His temper would flare when he became angry then quickly went dormant, back under his control. He was the opposite of Owen, who would viciously attack when he became angry and wouldn't be appeased until whatever had caused his anger lay broken and destroyed.

"We don't need kids; they just make a mess, according to Greer. Or we can adopt."

Her hand went to his wrist to remove it from her neck. "We've only known each other a few days; I think it's too soon to discuss children."

Slowly and methodically, he backed her into a dark corner until her back was against the wall. "You're the one who brought kids up first. I'm not going to deny it nearly broke me when you said you can't have children as if it's no big thing. It is a big thing, and I'm sure, in the future, we're going to cry about it a lot. I wanted to see your belly swell with my child, hold a baby only we could create, see you nursing our baby. Instead, I will get to see you holding our child, who we will pick out together, and watch as you feed him a bottle. The memories and love we will create don't depend on whether our child shares our DNA."

Every word he spoke sparked a fire in the part of her groin that she had assumed no one could make her burn for their touch. The man she had gone out with in her lone attempt to join the dating world had left her passionless and had her wanting to run and wash his taste from her lips.

Her hands were pressed against the wall behind her neck, where she had been trying to remove his. She quit trying now, hers going pliant. There was only one way to find out what she needed to know. Them being soul mates was an impossibility —they didn't exist—and if they did, soul mates were made for other women, not her. Not a woman who had been born under a gray cloud.

"Kiss me, Matthew."

Matthew dropped his eyes to her mouth. Alanna could have sworn she saw a flame behind his eyes before he covered her lips with his.

Instantaneous combustion had her knees buckling, and if Matthew's body weren't pressed against hers, she would have slipped to the floor. He moved his mouth over hers with the sensuality of man who had been wanting a taste of something inaccessible, and now that it was within his grasp, he was going to linger and savor.

Turning her hands in his grasp, she held on for dear life when he slid his tongue into her mouth to twirl and dance with hers in an erotic symphony that had her hips unconsciously seeking to mold her body to his.

Every nerve in her lower body was on fire, spreading heat throughout her. She started shaking, as if she had just come down with a flu. Then she realized it wasn't the result of sickness, but something she had never experienced before and hadn't been able to recognize as to what was going on in her body.

Desire.

It was the urgent need to give him whatever he wanted and to take every single thing she wanted from him until they were fused together in every way possible.

Matthew pulled his mouth away from hers to slide it down her neck, his tongue touching her erratic pulse.

"You taste like sunshine," she was able to get out once she had enough oxygen to spare.

"How does sunshine taste?" he murmured.

"Like a blood orange. Citrusy. The longer you kissed me, the more it made me think of an orange grove on a sunny day."

"Do you want to know how you taste?"

Uncomfortable, she nodded, not used to exchanging sweet talk with anyone, much less a man who looked as if he were an over six-foot-three living, breathing Greek statue.

"You taste as if you swiped one of those little bottles of honey we got yesterday."

"I didn't swipe it. Silas gave me one."

"God bless him," he moaned, lifting his head to smother her again.

Alanna couldn't help it; she started laughing. Her laughter was short-lived, though, before she was caught back in the golden glow of the fire that was consuming them. Matthew released her hands to slide his under her thin sweater.

"Dammit," he swore, breaking away from her.

Her arms, which had been clutching his shoulders, were now clutching air. Embarrassed, she dropped them back to her sides. He didn't want her after all …

With his hand, he bracketed her chin. "I stopped because your sweater is wet, not because I wanted to. I don't want you to get sick."

She frowned, not quite believing him. "I was pressed against your chest; how did you not feel it until you touched it?"

He gave a wry smile. "Because you have me so hot that I didn't notice. My hands are more sensitive when something is wet."

The strangeness of what he was saying had her believing him. Why would his hands be so sensitive to something wet? Understanding dawned. Maybe they had been burned badly in the past from working at his forge.

Goose bumps rose on her arms. Shivering, she crossed her arms over her chest.

"You're freezing." Matthew moved to where there were three stacked bins. Lifting one, he set it down on the ground then snapped off the lid. "We keep some of our extra winter clothes stored here." Sifting through several shirts and sweaters, he selected a gray and black flannel and handed it to her. "Here, change into this." Going back to the bin, he continued to rummage through the clothes.

Hastily switching tops, she quickly buttoned the flannel shirt and fell in love with the heated warmth.

"How is it so warm?" Rubbing her cheek against the warm material, she watched Matthew shrug into a dark blue hoodie.

"The bin was against the wall where the sun is shining outside. It must have heated them." Closing the bin, he set it back on top, turned around, and rubbed his hands together. "Let's get started."

Did he mean resume where they had left off?

She was getting ready to tell him that she wasn't ready for more when he lifted a bushel of apples to place it by the door.

"I'll take them to Ginny when we get the rest of the stuff organized."

Pfft. Kissing was no longer on his mind. Why was she so piqued he was able to switch off so easily from their heated embrace?

She stiffly picked up one of the bags containing the pie fillings. "Where do these go?"

After showing her, he went back to retrieve the other two bags. Together, they made short work of organizing the purchases. Matthew even made a bag of items she had picked out for her to take back to her trailer.

He carried the bushel of apples as they left the storage building and set it outside to give her an apple.

"Hold on to that while I get the trough. We can give it to your cow."

"Okay." Walking back to the pen, she talked to the cow, who was staring at her without interest.

"You were much more sociable yesterday." Her fingers itched to pat the tufts of white on top of the cow's head.

Seeing Matthew coming, carrying the heavy trough, she opened the gate for him. Once it was placed, he filled it with water.

"What you going to name her?"

"I can name her?"

"Since she won't be on the dinner table, might as well," he teased.

"Then I want to name her Molly."

"I'm surprised you didn't choose Buttercup."

"Oh ... That might be better." She gave the name a considering thought.

"Too late. Stick with the first one. It suits her better, especially since she won't be giving us any butter either."

"Quit dissing my cow. You'll hurt her feelings."

Matthew shook his head at her. "Just make sure you don't wear red around her. Cows don't like red."

"I didn't know that."

"Yeah, they can't stand it."

"Then I'll make sure I don't. Is there anything else I should know about them?"

"Yeah." His lips twitched as he gave Molly the apple. "Stock up on bug repellent."

Chapter Twenty-Four

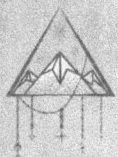

Alanna closed the door to Jody's home, finally done for the day. She was in a rush to get home to shower and change before Matthew came over for dinner. She had made a new Crock-Pot recipe for them to try out. The last two had been hit or miss.

She entered the trailer and started taking her shirt off before she was out of the living room. She had spent too long talking to Ginny and had been playing catchup ever since.

After she removed the rest of her clothes, she stepped into the shower. The last month had flown by with her spending most of her free time with Matthew. Usually, he would show up at dinnertime, and afterward, they would take a long walk, holding hands. Then they would settle down to watch a movie or just sit and talk with music playing.

Each day, she felt as if her head was in a guillotine, and she was just waiting for the blade to drop. She had never been happier in her life. Her smile slipped, worried about the call she'd received from Diamond.

Her lawyer was meeting her at Silas' house in the morning to discuss her case. Alanna was sure she was going to be given her court date. The thought of going to court not only terrified her because she might lose her freedom, but also potentially having to end her budding relationship with Matthew.

Each evening they spent together, their kissing sessions had become longer and more intense, leaving them both shaking and their breathing labored. She kept putting the brakes on them moving their relationship to a different level of intimacy.

She couldn't bring herself to have sex with Matthew until she was free of the court case, Owen, and, more importantly, Kate. If Kate found out she was in love with Matthew, she would somehow use it against her. That was what Kate did, with ruthless disregard of the carnage left behind.

Dressing in soft-as-butter jeans, she tugged on a robin-egg blue sweater, which was the same color as her jeans. After putting on socks, she went to the small kitchenette to make a salad to go along with the Crock-Pot lasagna.

The smell coming from the Crock-Pot had her stomach grumbling. All she had eaten was a sandwich at Ginny's house.

A rap at her door had her hurrying to answer it. Matthew was standing outside with a platter of cookies that had clear wrap over them.

"Those look familiar to me." Moving aside, she let him in.

"I don't know what you're talking about." Matthew carried the purloined cookies to the small table where she had placed the salad.

"I mean, I saw Ginny making a batch of cookies for Gavin to take The Last Riders."

Unashamedly, he pulled the cling wrap back to take out one of the humongous peanut butter cookies. "The Last Riders don't need them. They get freshly baked goods every day—one of the members is married to the town's best baker. Ginny used to work for her."

"I should have paid more attention to her recipe, then. I didn't know you liked cookies."

"There isn't a man alive who doesn't like cookies. By the way, she's making cowboy cookies on Saturday. They're my favorite, in case you just want to drop by unexpectedly when she's making them." His boyish grin melted her heart. She knew where she would be spending part of her Saturday.

She dipped out the lasagna into a serving bowl and set it down on the table.

"An Italian restaurant couldn't have done better," he complimented her. "All we need are some candles."

"Ask, and you shall receive." Alanna went back to the kitchen to pull out a small drawer and take out a long white candle and the tiny holder for it.

Matthew raised an eyebrow when she set it down on the table. "When did you buy a candle?"

"I didn't." She smiled, taking a seat at the table. "I found it in the drawer when I was searching for oven mitts. Jacob must have bought it for when he had a date over."

Matthew shot that assumption down. "More like he bought it for when the generator goes out."

Alanna dipped a large lasagna portion onto his plate before serving herself a smaller amount.

"Do you have your lighter on you?"

"Yes ... Do I smell bread?"

"Oh ... I almost forgot." Hopping up from the table, she went to the stove to take out the garlic bread. "I almost burnt it." Placing the toast on a plate, she brought it to the table, seeing the candle was lit.

"Thank you for lighting the candle."

"No problem."

After they ate, they did the dishes together then went on their nightly walk. As they did, they stopped by Molly's pen to feed her the last apple.

Alanna turned her head and saw Moses walking with his dogs.

"He has a real affinity to them, doesn't he?"

"Yes," Matthew said, turning to look at where she was staring.

Alanna turned back to Matthew. "That reminds me. When are you going to let me see your house? Moses broke and let me tidy up his place yesterday. Come on; I promise I won't be shocked at whatever shape it is in."

Matthew leaned back against the fence to stare at her. "You think I haven't showed you my place because I'm a slob?"

"I'm not saying slob, per se." Teasing him, she bumped his arm with her shoulder. "Come on ... I promise I won't be a judgmental bitch."

A myriad of expressions crossed his face before he gave her a worried look. "I'm going to hold you to that."

She became worried at the way he was acting when he didn't take her hand as they resumed walking.

The direction was the same as his other brothers', yet farther back, so they walked on the back dirt road, which was another entry from the main road.

"This way." Matthew led her up a small rise that blocked the view from the road they were walking on. He hesitated when they came close enough that she could see the shape of a house beyond three massive trees.

"Matthew, we don't have to go inside if you don't want to show me."

"No." His mouth firmed. "I want you to see all of it."

As they walked closer, she was able to catch sight of his house. It was larger than Silas'. The house facing them was a blue and white two-story house. A porch wrapped around to the back and out of sight. Two rocking chairs were sitting on the porch, just waiting to be filled. Struck by the beauty of

Matthew's house, she started taking in the yard and noticed a swing attached to two trees. There was even a small picket fence with huge planters filled with orange mums. It was the small picket fence, though, that poked at a long-ago memory.

"When I grow up and get married ..." Her voice cracked as she remembered telling the wind the same birthday wish she'd had for several years until the wind had stopped talking to her. "I'm going to have a blue and white two-story house, with a swing in the front yard so I can watch my children play, two rockers so when my husband and I get old, we can sit there and watch the night sky." Alanna turned toward Matthew. "And I wanted a blue picket fence around the house."

"How did I do?" he asked hoarsely.

Alanna stared at him in dismay. "How did you know this is the house I dreamt of having some day? I never told anyone."

Matthew shoved his hands in his back pockets. "Do you like it?"

"*Like* isn't a strong enough word. I love it."

"I just finished it before you came. Do you want to see inside?"

"Oh yeah ..." She could barely contain her enthusiasm.

Watch yourself, Alanna, she warned herself.

She walked through the door and was awestruck by the hardwood floors. Unlike Ginny's home, it didn't have all modern appliances. Alanna lovingly ran her hand over the vintage red reconditioned stove.

She gave a low whistle. "I've only seen one of these in a house I was selling. The buyer wanted to include it in the sale of the house, and the owner wanted over five grand for it. Needless to say, the buyer didn't get it."

"It was in Dad's house before he bought a new one. It was sitting in the storage building. I had it reconditioned."

"It's beautiful. I can see why you prefer working with this

rather than having me dump something in the Crock-Pot for you."

"I love your Crock-Pot meals."

She rolled her eyes at him. "I know I'm not a great cook. That's okay. I'm getting better."

"Yes, you are. You want to see the upstairs?"

As they went up the staircase, she stared down at the empty living room.

"You haven't gotten around to picking out furniture?"

"No, I've been waiting."

"For what?"

"You."

Chapter Twenty-Five

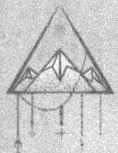

Matthew could tell from her wry smile that she thought he was kidding.

On the landing, he opened one of the six bedroom doors, letting her glance inside each empty room. He had put a lot of thought into making the home comfortable for all the children he planned to have. There was still an ache inside his chest, but after the last month, he didn't feel as if there was a gaping wound that would never be filled. She was meant for him. Whatever trials and tribulations they would go through in their lives ahead, they could overcome. Once they cleared the first hurdle ... of him confessing his family's gifts.

This could go badly. However, he was determined to tell her tonight. Ezra and Fynn both warned him over the last two days that a dark day lay ahead, and they couldn't see beyond today. That meant something was going to happen tomorrow that could change the direction of Alanna and his future.

Silas had come by his shop after Alanna left his house, telling him that Diamond had scheduled a meeting with Alanna tomorrow. Whatever Diamond had to talk to her about must be what Ezra and Fynn had been warning him.

He had saved the middle room facing the front yard for last. Opening the door after Alanna had checked out the others, he let her go in first. She gave him a surprised glance from over her shoulder when she saw it was the only one that had furniture.

"Ezra made the bed."

The huge four-poster bed was made out of dark cherry wood, with swirling patterns carved at the top of the headboard and bottom.

Alanna went to the headboard to run her hand over the swirling pattern. "I've never seen anything like this. It's gorgeous."

Looking up, she saw a mirror hanging over the bed. All his brothers, and Ginny, had the same type of mirror. "Your brothers have a mirror like this in their places."

"Each one is different."

Alanna looked back at the mirror. "How?"

"Each mirror is an image of what the stars looked like the night we were born."

"That's cool." Moving to the window, she pulled the cream curtain aside to look out.

Matthew wished he could read her mind. Her expression had turned melancholy.

"Mrs. Bates is coming tomorrow to talk to me."

Matthew came to stand behind her, winding his arms around her waist and pulling her into his chest. "Are you frightened about what she wants to tell you?"

"If it were good news, she would have told me over the phone."

"Not necessarily," he disagreed. "She might want to see your face when she tells you good news."

"Maybe." She didn't sound convinced.

"Let's not worry about it tonight."

"I'm down with that." She turned in his arms. "You ready to go back to my place to watch a movie?"

"I'm movie'd out. There are only so many zombie movies I can watch. Besides, it's gotten dark, and I don't have a flashlight."

A mischievous glint entered her eyes. "Mr. Coleman, did you bring me here to seduce me?"

Matthew tilted her head back so he could look into her clear eyes. The shadows weren't entirely gone, but they were filled much more often with happiness and merriment.

"*You* asked to come here. I'm the one who should be looking for ulterior motives. Are *you* planning on seducing me?" Kissing the corner of her lips, he pulled back teasingly when she turned her head, trying to capture the kiss, and clicked his tongue at her.

"Nuh-uh ... Do you think I'm easy?" he chided her as he took her hands and slowly walked her backward toward the bed.

The room was practically pitch black; only the glow of the moonlight outside the window gave a small portion from total obscurity. Tumbling backward onto the bed, he pulled her on top of him.

"Now, isn't this better than necking on a tiny couch?" He gave an exaggerated groan as they sank into the mattress.

"The couch isn't that small."

A ray of moonlight gave Alanna's face an ethereal glow.

He grew serious. Any desire to tease her had evaporated.

"Do you know how much I love you?"

Her beautiful face grew solemn. "Don't say that ..."

"Why?"

Alanna buried her face in his neck, her hand going to his chest. "Just don't."

"You're going to have to give more of an explanation than

that. I love you, and you hiding your face won't make it go away as if I never said it."

He loved Alanna with every part of his being, but when she was frightened, she tended to ignore the obvious, just as she had when he had replicated her dream home from what she had told Silas.

"You haven't known me long enough to know what you feel for me."

"Couples have gotten married after one week of knowing each other and have been very happy. We've been seeing each other for over a month. Hell, we've quadrupled our chances of having a happy marriage."

Alanna raised her head. "Are you asking me to marry you?"

"Yes. Do you want me to get on my knees?" He moved his hands to her shoulders, as if he was going to toss her off him. Instead, he gently rolled her over until he was above her.

"Let's wait until we make any plans. I don't know what Mrs.—"

"I don't care what Diamond wants to talk about. It won't make any difference to the way I feel about you. Would it change the feelings you have for me?"

"No ... Matthew, if anything happened to you because of me, I'd never get over it. I told you Owen and Kate are dangerous,"

Alanna had told her how Owen and Kate had tormented her throughout her childhood. She still hadn't gone through specifics as to as why she couldn't have children, but he knew they both bore the responsibility.

"I can take care of myself. They are the ones who should be worried about me. Kentucky men will kill for their woman, and you're mine regardless of whether you let me put a ring on your finger or not. You. Are. Mine."

He could see the fear in her eye.

"Don't think about them tonight, please," he begged.

"They're always there, no matter what I do."

"One day, they will not be, I promise." He gently lowered his mouth to cover hers. "Every time you think of them, imagine me standing in front of you, protecting you. I'll never let them get past me. They *won't* get past me."

She didn't respond at first, her lips trembling under his. He could feel her fear of them. Slowly, he released the control he kept over his body, allowing him to gradually raise his body temperature until her shaking body would absorb the heat coming from his. Carefully maintaining the temperature, he gave her soothing warmth.

"All I want you to do is repeat after me ..." He moved his hands under the soft material of her sweater to feel the heated warmth of her silky skin.

"I ..." he started.

"I ..." she repeated.

"Love ..."

"Love ..."

"You."

"You."

"Now say it all together," he instructed.

"I love you."

"See? That wasn't too hard to say, was it?" Matthew trailed his lips down her neck as he inched his hands higher.

"No, it was very easy. You're very loveable, Matthew."

Moving his hips to the side so she wouldn't feel his straining cock trying to strangle itself to get out of his jeans, he gritted his teeth to prevent himself from pushing her too far too fast. He wanted to make love to her slowly, to create a special memory that would replace the terror-filled ones that haunted her.

Raising her sweater over her bra-covered breasts, he held her eyes as he pulled it over her head and arms. Sliding his tongue between her parted lips, he slowly melded their lips together. At the same time, he caressed the sensitive skin on the side of her breast, using the pads of his thumbs. Matthew wanted her mind on the sensations he was creating within her, to find beauty in the memory he wanted to gift them both with.

His chest constricted when her body became pliant under his, as she wound her arms around his neck to hold him tighter.

"I love you, Alanna. I don't need months and years to decide what my feelings are for you."

Matthew left her moist lips to trail along the valley between her breasts. "These are the only two breasts I want to touch." He placed a tiny kiss on the side of each mound. "That I've ever touched or will touch."

Matthew felt her hand move to the back of his head to pull it up so she could search his eyes. "Are you saying ...?"

Mathew stared back at her forthrightly. "Most men don't want to admit they're virgins, but I am." He smiled down at her shocked expression. "How could I make love to the woman I loved when she wasn't here?"

Tenderly, she rubbed her cheek against his. "I would have never guessed," she said against his cheek.

"I want to be completely honest with you. There is something else I need to tell you about me, about my family, that I should have told you before."

Alanna wiggled underneath him. "Can it wait? I'm still preoccupied with you being a virgin."

His lips twitched in amusement. "Is it such a big shocker?"

She slid her silky hands over his shoulders. "Oh yeah ... My hands have gone where no woman has before."

"Or will," he promised her.

"Even better."

Her mouth curved into a smile he couldn't resist kissing. The passion he had been holding back burst from him as he stroked the roof of her mouth with his tongue. Sliding her bra straps down, he unfastened the bra between her breasts. It was Alanna who pulled it off and tossed it aside to bury her nipples into his chest.

A hiss of a sigh escaped him as her cool flesh touched his heated warmth. She was wreaking havoc on his control over his temperature. He had to remember that she could be hurt if he wasn't careful.

Resolved to making their first experience memorable, he stroked her body like a new piece of iron, to discover the strength and design he wanted to give it. Rising up, he slowly peeled her jeans and panties off. Then, lying back down, he placed his hand on her trembling belly.

"I would never hurt you, Alanna."

"I know ... I don't know why I'm shaking."

"I do ..." he murmured, scooting down to place butterfly kisses over her belly. "You're waiting for me to strike out at you. I'm not. I would rather incinerate myself."

Laughter bubbled out from her throat. "Dramatic much?"

Sensing her fear had subsided, he moved to lie between her legs. Kissing her inner thighs, he spread her legs wider, parting the cleft of her pussy. He slid his tongue along her thigh, upward to her mound, curling his tongue around her vulva. He held her hips down when she arched under him. He didn't want to lose the treasure he had just found.

Savoring her taste like a fine wine, he played with his treasure before letting his tongue dip into the cavern below.

Her moist pussy welcomed him with her muscles clenching around his tongue. Sliding his tongue higher, he stroked the sides as Alanna writhed under his mouth.

Building her desire, like he would gradually increase the

flames in his forge, he stroked her channel until she was whimpering and moaning. He stroked and sucked on her opening until he felt her climaxing on his tongue.

Removing his tongue, he gently slid his cock inside while she was still spasming with her orgasm.

"There's no way you haven't done that before," she gasped out.

Clenching his teeth because it was impossible for him to speak at the sensations assailing him, he laid his head on her shoulders to ease the constriction in his chest. He felt as if he was going to burst into flames inside of her. Thank heaven the moistness would keep him from spontaneously combusting, or he would be a goner. They both would be.

The chilling thought had him regaining his self-control enough to move within her.

"There is nothing like this in the whole world."

She gazed up at him tenderly. "I'm thinking the same thing. There's no one like you in this whole world. I didn't even know men like you could exist."

Her words had him about to confess that she didn't know how true her words were.

"Alanna, I *am* different. My whole family is ..."

As he talked, she started moving, driving his cock to the hilt inside of her. His mind turned to molten lava. All mental functioning went haywire, leaving his body to instinctively take over, to drive his cock inside of her as fast and deep as he could go. Shaking, he tried to draw it out longer, determined not to come yet, but when she wound her legs around his hips to match his movements, his willpower evaporated, leaving only the driving need to reach the ultimate completion of showing his love for her.

Collapsing on top of her, he started to roll off her, not wanting to smother her with his weight. Alanna tightened her arms around him, though, refusing to let him go.

"You may have just convinced me to marry you. If we're this good the first time"—she gave a shaky laugh—"it's only going to get better, right?"

Matthew relaxed his damp body on hers.

"Do they make fireproof mattresses?" he asked when he could get his vocal cords to work.

"I'm sure. Why?"

"We're going to need one."

Chapter Twenty-Six

Alanna was practically skipping. After spending the rest of the night with Matthew in his bed, she had managed to drag her sore body out at the crack of dawn. They had walked back to her trailer, where she had showered and changed into jeans and the gray and black flannel shirt Matthew had given her the day they had splashed water onto each other.

After eating bowls of cereal, they walked together to his shop, holding hands.

"Isaac and I are helping Jody and Jacob set up a new gate a few miles from here, but I'll be back before Diamond gets here," he promised.

"You don't have to rush. I don't want you hurrying the job. I'll be fine—"

"I *want* to be here," he insisted. "I just don't want you getting anxious about what she has to say. Whatever it is, good or bad, we'll deal with it."

"I'm glad you're confident, because I'm not." Nervous, her stomach was rolling just thinking of the upcoming meeting.

"Don't be nervous." Taking her hands, he warmed them between his. Alanna leaned into his warmth.

"That's easier said than done." Forcing a smile to her lips, she gave him a quick kiss before pulling away at hearing footsteps crunching over branches. Turning, she saw Isaac coming from his place.

"You ready?" Isaac's voice traveled over.

"I better be getting to work." Flushing, she hurried away, embarrassed when she saw Isaac staring at the red mark she had accidently left on Matthew's neck.

At Silas' house, she quickly started the pork chop Crock-Pot meal Silas wanted. Unloading the dishwasher didn't take long. Neither did making a fresh pot of coffee after pouring herself one. She normally didn't drink coffee, but she hadn't slept much last night and could use the extra boost.

After spending the rest of the morning doing chores at Matthew's brothers' places, she made a brief stop at her place to take a couple of steaks out of the freezer. Matthew had promised her that they could grill them on the firepit tonight, joking that he would call and make sure Greer was working before starting the fire.

Ginny had lunch ready for them when she arrived at her place. After they ate the chicken salad, Ginny left her to take a quick nap. Gavin, Freddy, and Ginny were going to an Easter party at one of The Last Riders' member's houses. Easter wasn't until Sunday, but they were having a party tonight so the children could have an egg decorating contest.

She watched the clock, and about half an hour before Ginny was supposed to wake, Alanna gave Freddy a bath and changed him.

"You are so adorable," she crooned, picking him up. She was packing him out the bathroom when Ginny came out her bedroom. It took her a minute to realize she had dressed him in his Easter suit already.

She carried Freddy out to Ginny's car for her, watching as they drove away. She checked the cell phone Silas had loaned her and headed back to his house. She should make it just before Mrs. Bates arrived.

She was relieved to see there were no cars in Silas' driveway, meaning she had made it in time.

As she was going up the side steps to Silas' home, Matthew and Isaac pulled in.

Grinning, Matthew hopped out of the car. "I told you I'd make it in time."

"I knew you would," she assured him, as he and Isaac came up the steps.

Matthew opened the door for her to go inside.

"Anyone want a cup of coffee?" Silas asked as he came down the stairs.

"No, thanks."

"I do," Isaac said. "I can get it if you want one." He headed toward the kitchen.

Silas followed him, leaving her and Matthew in the living room.

Taking her hand, he tugged her down onto one of the two couches that stood on opposite sides of the room, facing each other.

"Diamond's here," came from the kitchen as Silas carried two cups, handing one to Matthew.

Alanna waited breathlessly for the knock, terrified Mrs. Bates would tell her that they would try the case in Ohio, where Elizabeth had been kidnapped, or that she was given a court date. She knew she was innocent, but proving it with so much evidence against her wasn't a forgone conclusion.

Silas opened the door at the knock as Isaac came out of the kitchen.

Alanna stood when Diamond walked in the door, with

Elizabeth walking in behind her and a deputy whom Alanna recognized at Rod MacNeil.

Deputy MacNeil closed the door.

Alanna didn't know how to react to the unexpected sight of Elizabeth. Then Elizabeth saw her and broke into tears, running toward Alanna.

"I'm so sorry I lied," she sobbed. "I was so afraid ..."

Alanna immediately broke at seeing the woman she had loved from a young child. Reaching out to hug her, Alanna patted her back, trying to get Elizabeth to stop crying so hard. "I knew you were."

"I should have told you that Mom contacted me when we moved to Ohio. That's why I moved out. I didn't want to take the chance she would hurt you."

"It's okay."

"No, it's not. Please forgive me?"

"Of course." Alanna soothed her as she looked toward Mrs. Bates. "Does this mean ...?"

Diamond nodded. "We just came from the sheriff's office, where Elizabeth gave a statement of what really happened when she was kidnapped by Owen."

"I told the sheriff you had nothing to do with my kidnapping, that Owen forced me to give him your realtor code for the homes you were showing."

A buzzing sound had everyone looking around.

"Excuse the interruption." Silas took his cell phone out of his pocket, leaving the room to head into the kitchen as he put the phone to his ear.

Alanna felt a huge weight lift off her shoulders. "You knew who Owen was when you were kidnapped?"

Elizabeth pulled out of her arms. "I'm sorry I lied when you would ask me about him. Mom threatened to never let me see you again if I did."

"I wish you had told me. I would never have let you go

back to her. I shouldn't have, anyway." Self-recriminations were filling her as Silas came rushing in from the kitchen.

"That was Gavin on the phone. The school bus that Fynn was on was run off the road by a speeder who didn't see the stop sign out when Greer's nephew was let off. The bus rolled down the mountain with the kids on board!"

Silas snatched his car keys off the table. Isaac stood up from the table, as well as Matthew.

"Matthew, you stay here with Alanna and text Jody and Jacob to leave the job they're finishing. Isaac, you take Matthew's truck to round up Ezra and Moses."

Matthew tossed Isaac the truck keys, which he caught while rushing out of the dining room.

"Call as soon as you find something out," Matthew called out to them as they left.

Deputy MacNeil's radio started beeping. Alanna and the rest of them listened as the sheriff's voice came through the radio, calling the deputy and Diamond to the station so the car could be used to block the traffic coming up the mountain.

"Roger. We'll be on our way." The deputy opened the door. "We need to leave. Mrs. Bates, Ms. Easton."

"Of course. Alanna, I'll motion for the charges to be dropped, and you should have that contraption off your ankle by the afternoon."

"Thank you," she said to their backs as Deputy MacNeil ushered them out of the house.

Once they left, her lips trembled in worry for Fynn. "You should go. I'll be fine here."

"I'm not leaving you alone. The whole town is probably already there, helping out."

"Are you sure?"

"Yes. I'm sure Fynn is okay. Fynn is tough. He's used to us tossing him around like a football when he was little."

Matthew tugged her into his arms. "Hey, don't worry. We should be happy. The case against you is going to be dropped."

Alanna knew he was trying to relieve their worry by being positive.

"I'm going to get the marshmallows. We can go ahead and start the firepit, and you can start roasting the marshmallows while I get the steaks from your place."

"I don't want any. I'm afraid I'll choke on them right now ... until I know Fynn is all right."

He grabbed her arms. "He's okay. Ezra would have known if something bad was going to happen."

"How would Ezra have known?"

Matthew's face settled into a firm expression. "Let me get the marshmallows, start the firepit, and when I come back from getting the steaks, we're going to have a talk."

She nodded, her stomach sinking. Was he going to come up with some excuse for them not to get married now that she was practically free of the charges against her? Would he want her to return to Ohio?

The different possibilities were still running through her mind when he returned with the marshmallows. Silently, she walked alongside him to the firepit, her mind in turmoil with worry about Fynn and Matthew wanting to backpedal on their relationship.

She jumped when he placed a chair several inches away from the firepit. She hadn't noticed him getting the chairs from the outdoor shed.

Taking her by the shoulders, he sat her down. Numbly, she stared up at him.

"I won't be five minutes. Remember, there's a bucket by the cooling barrel, if you need it. Do not—I repeat: do not—dare roast one marshmallow until I'm back."

She couldn't help but smile at his foreboding expression.

"I promise."

"You better not," he warned with a finger pointed at her.

She stuck her tongue out at him, and Matthew bent over, catching her mouth in a kiss before she could pull it back. Grinning, he pulled away.

"That's better." He grinned, giving her a sexy wink, which relieved most of her fear.

She was unable to take her eyes off his sexy stride as he walked away toward her trailer. Looking around on the ground for a stick to use to roast the marshmallows with, she saw a couple, but that would have involved her getting up, which she had promised Matthew she wouldn't do.

She brought her eyes back to the firepit when her cell phone buzzed, showing she had a text message. She opened the phone and went to her text messages, and her blood turned cold when she read it.

Run, bitch. I'm counting to ten, and then I'm coming for you.

Chapter Twenty-Seven

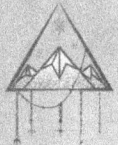

Alanna jumped up from the chair, staring down at her phone. She was given to the count of ten to hide.

The silly childhood game had been turned into a nightmarish match of wits between her and Kate. If she won, the night was spent cowering in fear of being caught until the sun rose in the morning. If Kate won, she would drag her to Owen's room to let him abuse her while she played look-out for their foster parents.

When Kate had started forcing her to play the game, she had invariably lost until one night she tried to climb out her bedroom window, uncaring if she would be hurt if she fell. Truthfully, she had reached the point of not caring if she survived. Anything was better than Owen hurting her the way he got a sick pleasure out of doing to her.

She climbed out of the window and was partially out when she heard the wind tell her to go back in.

Staring down at the concrete patio below, she pushed herself out farther, determined not to let Kate find her. Her time was running out, and she was just imagining the voice ... until she heard it again.

I'll help you hide. Leave the window open.

Climbing back inside like the wind told her to, she snuck downstairs and hid under Mrs. Fields's piano. She had never tried to hide downstairs.

She made it through the night unscathed. That was the first time she had won against Kate. She didn't always win. Sometimes, Kate cheated by not counting when she didn't do something Kate wanted done, but she was winning more than she had lost, especially when she started leaving a window open in her room.

It was only after, when Mrs. Fields had grown concerned about her not starting her period and contacted her case manager, that the reason she hadn't revealed the extent of abuse she had suffered at Kate's and Owen's hands. Because Kate and Owen were both minors when the attacks occurred, the details of what they had done to her had been sealed by the courts. Subsequently, they sent her to counseling, where the therapist told her it was her mind who had made up the wind talking to her. She took the medicine the therapist had prescribed, and the wind had stopped talking to her.

Sometimes she thought she could hear the voice in the wind talking to her, but it was so faint that she couldn't make it out. Gradually, she had stopped trying to listen. In jail, without her medicine, she had started hearing it again the night Matthew was arrested. Frightened that she was taking a backward step into a traumatic period in her life, she had resumed taking the medicine. Then she stopped taking it the next day, when she had seen the hurt in Matthew's eyes at her behavior.

Precious seconds were ticking away ... She frantically spun in place, determining where to hide. Matthew should be back any minute ... she didn't want him searching for her if Kate was coming for her.

"What should I do?" she screamed out, grabbing her head.

Hide in the fort. Matthew is coming.

She ran to the Coleman's childhood fort and had to bend and wiggle through the overgrown ivy clinging to the structure. Losing precious seconds so no one would see the ivy had been disturbed, she managed to crawl inside, ignoring the spiderweb clinging to her face. She waited until she was sitting in the farthest, darkest corner before removing the clinging web.

"Alanna, where are you? This is Deputy Huxley. The sheriff sent me to bring you to his office."

Don't listen. He isn't a deputy.

Through a gap in some stacked logs, Alanna could make out a uniformed leg. It was the same uniform that Deputy MacNeil had worn and that she had seen on the officers when she was in jail.

"I'm only here to help you ..."

"Who are you?"

Relief filled her at hearing Matthew's voice.

Stay quiet, the wind warned her.

Biting her fist, she remained silent, all the while wanting to run to Matthew.

"The sheriff sent me to protect Alanna."

"I know everyone who works for the police in town. You don't work there."

"I'm a new hire."

"Bullshit. Get off my property. If Knox wants to protect Alanna, he can either come himself or send Deputy MacNeil back."

"That might be hard to do." The deputy's voice had turned sinister. "Deputy MacNeil can't help himself right now. Hand her over and walk away."

"Get off my property."

Alanna had to scoot farther down on her bottom to get a better look, to make sure someone else hadn't arrived when Matthew's voice sounded just as sinister as the deputy's.

Damn. She had forgotten how scary he could sound when he wanted to.

She heard a rustling sound, and then the click of a gun.

"You should have walked away," the deputy snarled.

"You find her?"

Alanna brought her fist to her mouth to stifle any sound when she recognized Owen's voice.

"Not yet. There's been a holdup."

"Quit wasting time. Shoot him and help me look," Owen ordered.

Alanna saw Owen's jean-clad legs as he moved around outside the area, looking behind the firepit before coming back to where she was hiding.

"I know you're out here, Alanna. I searched the house, so you have to be out here somewhere. You know what I'm going to do when I find you, don't you?" he threatened. "Oh ... baby ... it's been a while since I've had you. I'm going to give it to you so hard—"

"You're not going to touch her!"

"Shoot him!"

"Dammit, I'm trying. The damn fire is blowing smoke in my eyes ..."

Alanna heard a sound of flesh meeting flesh and saw where Matthew had jumped toward the deputy to wrestle the gun away from his grip. Meanwhile, Owen continued searching the area, drawing closer to the fort. His only focus was her.

You're going to have to run when I tell you to.

Alanna shook her head frantically, too frightened to speak. Owen would see her if she crawled out of the fort.

He won't see you. The smoke will blind him enough for you to get a head start.

She began crawling to the opening of the fort, keeping to the side for as long as she could.

Run!

Her instinct was to go to Matthew, seeing him and the uniformed man struggling on the ground.

Jerking to her feet, she started toward them.

No! Run! We're on our way to help him.

She took off at a run, past the fort, then Matthew and Isaac's shop, hoping to reach the cover of the woods before Owen caught her.

Who's on the way? Her frantic thoughts didn't have a clue who was coming to help.

Hearing footsteps gaining ground on her, she couldn't help but turn her head to see how close Owen was getting to her, only to trip and fall over the small rise when she saw it was Elizabeth. Is she the one who the wind said was coming to help?

Don't stop! the wind howled at her. *She wants to hurt you, not help you!*

Disbelieving, she stood up, seeing Elizabeth had stopped chasing her and was edging closer to her.

"Come here, Alanna. I'll protect you."

Slowly, Alanna started to edge backward at the crazy look in Elizabeth's eyes. She shifted her gaze downward, to Elizabeth's hands. She was holding a bloody knife.

"Are you hurt?"

Elizabeth stepped closer, raising the bloody knife.

"No. I wasn't the one hurt." Elizabeth pulled the knife closer to her face to lick the blade. "It's not my blood."

Alanna took another step backward, unwilling to play cat and mouse with a woman whom she had adored since she herself was just a teenager.

"Whose blood is it?"

"Your lawyer's. Oh ... and the deputy's. The sheriff really

should make it a thing to look under the seats before letting people in his squad car. Any ole person could come along and hide one. Luckily for me, someone did."

Alanna didn't wonder who that person was. Kate.

"You hurt them?"

"Put it this way … the deputy has made his final arrest, and poor Mrs. Bates won't be defending anyone ever again. She chose the wrong person to represent when she chose you over me."

"Elizabeth … I don't understand. I love you. I tried to protect you—"

"From whom? My mother?" Elizabeth screamed at her. "She's the only one who understands me. You certainly didn't … I hated it when she made me stay with you …" Sneering laughter came from her lips. "You were even stupid enough to pay for my moving expenses to Ohio for that lame-ass job Mom wanted me to take. I couldn't wait to move out of that apartment … If I had to live there one more day, I would have—"

Elizabeth sprang at her suddenly, and Alanna quit trying to reason with her when she saw what lucidity Elizabeth had left was gone. She had let Elizabeth get too close to her. There was no way she would be able to outrun her.

Just then, she saw one of the Porters' signs and turned in the direction of their property.

Please let it be true! she screamed in her head. *Please let it be true that one of the Porters is watching.*

If Elizabeth was about to kill her, she wanted a witness to what had happened to her and Matthew, if he didn't survive either.

She had only gone ten steps before she ran headlong into a male chest.

"What the fuck are you doing—"

"She's going to kill me," Alanna managed to wheeze out. "I work for the Co—"

"I know who you are."

A deranged scream came toward them, and Alanna turned to look, seeing Elizabeth charging toward them with the large knife raised.

The man shoved her aside to raise the gun in his hand, firing a shot off in the same motion. Blood came gushing out of Elizabeth's chest as she was knocked backward to the ground.

Alanna took off running in the direction she had just come from.

"Where in the fuck are you going?"

"I have to help Matthew. They're going to kill him!" she screeched out, not stopping. She had to help Matthew, praying the man with the gun would follow her.

Hearing his footfalls and snapping branches, she ran faster.

Please let Matthew be all right. Please ...

She ran over the rise and saw Matthew getting off the fake deputy, who lay unmoving.

"What in the fuck did you do to him?"

Alanna stopped running when she heard the fear in Owen's voice and saw it on his face.

Matthew's back was turned to her, so he hadn't seen her coming to a stop a few feet away.

"I did to him exactly what I'm going to do to you."

She was still frozen in place when she saw Silas, Isaac, and Moses running up the driveway to encircle Owen.

Silas nodded at the man on the ground. "He's the one who ran the school bus off the road. We found Deputy MacNeil's car with the deputy and Diamond inside. The deputy was killed, and Diamond's being worked on at the hospital. They think she'll make it."

Thank God. Alanna started crying at hearing the woman wasn't dead.

"The road is blocked with everyone trying to get past where the emergency vehicles are trying to reach the bus. Jody, Jacob, and Ezra are with Fynn at the hospital. I think he's got a broken arm. Greer's nephew wasn't hurt. A little girl was pinned under the bus when it went down. She died." Silas' face was filled with hatred as he stared at Owen, who was just staring back at them. Owen might be a terror where women were concerned, but with men, he showed himself to be the coward he was.

"I was only trying to protect Alanna from Elizabeth."

"How did you know Elizabeth was here?" Matthew fired off the question without giving Owen a chance to talk. Then a spark of fire hit Owen in his chest.

"Where's your ankle monitor? You're supposed to be restricted to the hotel room your lawyer got for you. Where's all your big talk about what you were going to do to Alanna when you found her?"

As Matthew scornfully talked, sparks of fire keep hitting Owen, forcing him to start wildly patting his clothes.

"What in the fuck? How are you doing that? Stop! That hurts!" Owen yelled, trying to step away from Matthew.

With a low whistle, Moses's dogs ran out to growl at Owen. Every time Owen tried to move, one of the dogs would nip at him.

"I'm not hurting you one-tenth of what you did to Alanna!" Matthew's harsh voice had her shivering. "You turned an innocent game of hide and seek into terrorizing a small child, then you raped her, destroying any chance of her becoming a mother, or *me becoming their father*!"

Alanna still couldn't see Matthew's expression, but she could see when he raised his hand high in the air to point a finger at Owen. Then he began making a circle in the air. She watched in amazement as fire shot out from the tip of his finger to land on Owen. Then Matthew started moving his finger faster, going up and down.

Alanna watched, horror-stricken, as flames consumed a screaming Owen. The snapping dogs backed away as the fire devoured him within their depths, the fire swirling around him like a tornado of heat. Then Owen crumbled to the ground when Matthew turned his hand palm up and the flame flew to him as if Matthew had beckoned them like Moses his dogs. The flames danced on his hand until he closed it into a fist. When he opened his hand again, the flames were gone.

Alanna stood there, trying to grasp what had just happened. She must have lost her mind when she had seen Elizabeth shot, which was the only rational explanation she could come up with. It was the godawful smell coming from the burnt, still smoldering spot on the ground where Owen and the fake deputy should have been, but both were gone and that snapped her out of her thoughts.

A shrill sound had her coving her ears to drown out the noise that was so loud it was mind numbing.

"Alanna, stop screaming." Matthew surrounded her with his arms.

Frightened by what she had just witnessed, she tore herself out of his arms. "I've lost my mind. I didn't just see you burn—"

"Please don't be afraid of me." Matthew's grim visage turned heart wrenching. "I can explain—"

"How can you explain killing a man?"

"Because he wasn't a man. He was a monster who preyed on the innocent. He should have been locked up when the foster system found out he had raped two other girls, beside you. He should have never been put in a home where there were females, and they didn't even give your foster parents any clue what type of monster they had allowed into their home."

She stared down at the smoldering ground, the stench making her want to vomit. Gagging, she covered her mouth.

Matthew took her by the arm to move her away from the stench and toward Silas' home. Helping her sit down on the upper step, he used his hand to press her head down to her knees.

"Isaac, get her a glass of water." She heard Silas tell his brother.

Alanna felt Isaac hurry past her and heard the screen door open.

"Just breathe," Matthew said, sitting down next to her to put an arm around her.

"Greer and Dustin aren't answering my calls. Is Logan okay?"

"He is fine, Tate. He was already off the bus when it went over," Silas answered the man who had shot Elizabeth. "They're trying to get the bus stabilized before they can get more paramedics inside to help bring the other kids out."

"If you've got everything under control here, I'm going to help with the bus."

"We've got it. Tate, our family owes you." He gave the man a nod. "You'll have to walk. Traffic is lined up and down the mountain."

"I'll catch a ride back with Dustin or Greer. That's two. Don't think Greer isn't keeping count."

"He never lets me forget it," Silas said wryly.

Raising her head, she saw Tate about to move away, but then he paused.

"I expect one of you to take care of the woman in Greer's pot patch. Can't have Knox sniffing around."

"She'll be gone before you get back." Silas nodded.

Alanna felt as if she were in a never-ending nightmare,

where they were just casually standing around, talking like getting rid of a dead body was an everyday occurrence. Maybe it was. Maybe there had been so many horror movies about killers living on mountains for a reason.

Matthew taking the glass of water from Isaac to hand it to her had her flinching away. Scooting away from her, he set it down between them. "I would never hurt you."

She pressed her dry lips together, seeing the pain in his eyes.

"I wanted to tell you about my gift." Matthew looked up to stare at his brothers standing at the bottom of the steps. "What gifts we all have. I couldn't find the courage. I should have told you last night. I *tried* to tell you last night, but then I got distracted." Matthew's hands hung down between his thighs. "I'm a fire walker."

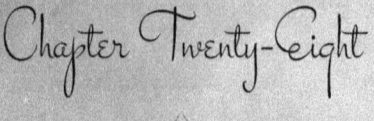

Chapter Twenty-Eight

S he shook her head. "Fire walkers don't exist."

"They do. I am one. I can create fire, walk through fire, and anything else you can imagine." Matthew turned his hand palm up. On the tip of his index finger, a tiny ball of fire appeared.

Alanna watched as he lifted each individual finger and moved them. The tiny ball jumped to each finger before returning to his index finger. As Matthew stared at it, it grew bigger and bigger until it was the size of a baseball then disappeared when he closed his fist, as if he had shut off the oxygen.

"I can control the way it moves."

"I saw that for myself." She shuddered.

"I can withstand high heat, which would—"

"Kill anyone else," she finished for him. "Saw that, too, or is my mind making it up?"

"You didn't imagine it. You've never imagined anything happening to you."

Her eyes widened. "How do you know what I imagined?"

"Alanna."

Silas' voice drew her attention to him.

"You didn't imagine the wind talking to you. It was me."

"That's impossible ..."

Silas went to stand next to a pile of leaves he was raking this morning when she had come to his house. He extended his hands, and the leaves started to rise from the ground in a conglomerate of colors. As he lowered his hands, the leaves fell to the ground as if they hadn't been disturbed.

"It was you who told me to hide when Kate and Owen wanted to play the game?" Confused, she stared at him. *How is anything like this possible?*

"Yes."

"You were the one who told me you knew who my prince ..." Alanna looked away from his smile to stare at Matthew.

Silas nodded when she stared back at him. "Ezra has the gift of reading the stars. He saw that Matthew and you are soul mates."

She rubbed her temple. This was unbelievable, but she had witnessed what Matthew and Silas could do.

"What can you do?" she asked, staring at Isaac.

Affronted, he stared back at her. "Our gifts aren't carnival tricks. They are gifts which have been passed down through generations in our family. We stay isolated on this mountain so no one learns about what we are capable of doing. Imagine being a fire walker, or a wind talker, when people believed in witchcraft. Imagine what people would do if they found out Ezra could read the stars like an open book, or Fynn, who carries all the gifts to be passed down to future generations. He has the sight to see into the future ... Do you know what would happen if people found out he knew who won a football game, what stocks would surge, and which would tank?"

"Easy," Matthew said sharply. "She's in shock and scared."

"Welcome to our world." Isaac gave her a sad smile. "There isn't a day we don't live in fear that, when Fynn goes to school, someone will notice his gift ..."

Fynn was still just a child ... The mental picture of someone using him to satisfy their greed had her chest constricting in fear.

Isaac nodded at her, knowing she was beginning to understand their fear.

"To answer your question"—his voice gentled—"I am a shadow walker. I can manipulate fire, not to the extent that Matthew can, but to use so I can walk in the shadows of the flames. Wherever there's a fire, past or present, I can be present without being seen, or if they can, all they'll see is my shadow."

"You can't go into the future?"

"No, not without paying a price. Our gifts come at a cost. I'm not a star gazer, nor do I have the sight. If I go into the future, and the fire goes out, I'll be trapped. I won't be able to come back."

Alanna turned to look at Matthew. "Will you have to pay a price for using your gift today?"

"No, the mountain is our domain. If I had used my power off this mountain, then I would have."

She licked her dry lips. Then, picking up the glass of water, she took several drinks. "When you, Isaac, said *cost*, I take it we aren't talking about money?"

"No, something bad will happen in our life as punishment."

She looked at Silas. "You helped me escape Kate and Owen numerous times." She was almost afraid to ask, "Did you have to pay for helping me?"

Matthew's face as he looked at Silas was filled with pure love.

"Silas' soulmate should have fallen in love with him long ago, but she hasn't. She's too consumed with her family to give herself the chance to get to know Silas and fall in love."

"The woman at the orchard." Alanna surmised.

Silas gave her pained smile of acknowledgement.

"At least this time, you helped me on the mountain."

"When we got Fynn off the bus and he told me what was going to happen here, I knew we wouldn't make it in time, that there were three of them. I reached out to Tate. If I hadn't, you would have been dead before Matthew could have reached you."

Alanna squeezed her eyes shut, understanding the pained expression on his face. He wouldn't be getting his soul mate anytime soon.

Opening her eyes, she looked toward Moses, whose lips quirked in amusement.

"My gift is nothing special. I can communicate with animals."

Alanna rolled her eyes at him describing his gift as nothing special. The dogs lying by his feet might look gentle now, but minutes before, they had looked like the hounds from hell.

"What are Jacob's and Jody's gifts?"

"I think that's enough revelations for one night."

"You know what, you're right." She stared at the males around her. "Are you sure I'm not going to wake in the morning and find this is all a dream?"

Isaac gave her a twisted smile. "At least you didn't say nightmare."

Turning her head, she looked toward the direction where Elizabeth was lying out of sight. She started to cry. "Elizabeth was going to kill me."

"Ezra and Fynn both knew something was going to happen today. Because the wreck involved Fynn, he wasn't allowed to see what it was," Matthew explained.

"Can you call and see how Fynn and Diamond are?"

"Fynn has been released with a broken arm and a temporary cast. He's on his way with Jody and Jacob. They're still stuck in the traffic."

She started crying harder. "That little girl is dead because Kate and Owen wanted me dead."

"Elizabeth is just as culpable. She had to have known the accident was planned. She used the opportunity to slit the deputy's throat when he was stopped in the traffic."

"He's dead, too?"

"Yes," Silas confirmed. "Diamond would have died, too, if we hadn't seen where the deputy must have pulled over when Elizabeth threatened Diamond with a knife in the back seat."

"Will they finally arrest Kate?" she asked.

"I don't know," Matthew answered, gingerly scooting over to sit next to her. "I guess, if the sheriff can prove she was in on the plan."

"She was the one who planned it. I'm sure, Matthew. Owen wouldn't tie his shoes without Kate's permission."

"I'll talk to Knox once he knows Diamond is okay."

None of them were safe until Kate was where she deserved to be. She should leave ...

"She won't go unpunished," Matthew promised her. "But making yourself a target to keep us safe isn't going to happen."

"How did you know what I was thinking?" She narrowed her eyes on him. "Are any of you mind readers?"

Matthew grinned. "Not yet, but we won't know until my brothers start having children."

Morosely, she wiped the tears she had shed for Elizabeth from her cheeks. "You won't ..."

Matthew gave her a tender smile. "You're my soul mate, Alanna. I love you. Besides"—he grew teasing—"all of my brothers have promised me their firstborn child."

His brothers' mouths flew open at his outlandish claim.

"We told you," Isaac reminded him, "that you can be the first to hold them."

Silas tilted his head to the side, as if he could hear something no one else could. "Moses, Isaac, come with me. Tate and Dustin are about to come home."

Alanna swallowed hard. "Don't burn her like you did Owen."

Silas gave her a gentle look. "We weren't going to. There's a cemetery where our family is buried. I thought we would bury her there. I'll make her a nice box."

Alanna held the tears for Elizabeth at bay. Her mind went to the mother whose arms would be empty tonight because of Elizabeth's actions instead. If Elizabeth had been aware of the plan, then Silas was right—she was just as culpable.

Matthew helped her to stand then led her into Silas' house. Sitting her at the table, he went to the kitchen and returned with a plate of rice from the Crock-Pot meal she had made for Silas.

"I can't eat." She started to push the small plate away.

"I just gave you some rice. Just take a few bites to settle your stomach."

Picking up the spoon he had brought her, she managed to take a couple of bites then placed the spoon back down. He was right; the rice had gotten the awful taste out of her mouth. However, when she realized it was Owen's smoking body she was breathing in, her stomach rolled.

Jerking out of her seat, she ran into the bathroom and threw up. Matthew followed her, dampening a towel and placing it around her neck as she heaved over the toilet.

"Breathe this in." Matthew held an open alcohol bottle next to her face. "It'll help."

She breathed in the fumes, and her stomach eased enough for her to straighten.

Pulling the washcloth from around her neck, she used it to wipe her face. The coolness eased the last of her heaves.

She lowered the cloth from her face. "Just promise me one thing."

"Anything," he said, tucking a strand of her hair behind her ear.

"Don't ever burn anyone near me again."

Matthew pretended to consider the promise. "I'll try not to."

The man she loved couldn't be serious for five minutes. Matthew would brighten even the cloudiest of days. He was the exact opposite of Greer.

"Do I want to know what has you smiling?"

"I was just thinking how you're always in a good mood, joking around, and always making everyone around you feel happy. You're kind of the opposite of Greer."

Matthew made a strange face at her.

"What?"

"Nothing."

She placed her hands on her hips threateningly. "What?"

"I don't suppose this would be the time to tell you that the Porters and the Colemans are cousins."

Epilogue

Against her better judgment, Alanna knocked on Ginny's door. She should have texted her that she wasn't feeling well today and take the afternoon off. If today wasn't her first day back at work after returning from her and Matthew's honeymoon, at a small bed and breakfast in the Caribbean, she would have. Just a couple of hours, then she would go home and make some soup to settle her queasy stomach. Had she picked up a traveling bug?

"Come in."

Hearing Ginny's voice, she opened the door and headed inside.

Standing behind the kitchen counter, Ginny took one look at her face and went to the cabinet to grab a cup. She poured some hot water into it then opened a box and grabbed a teabag, plopping it into the cup.

Alanna went to the long-legged barstool to sit next to Freddy's highchair.

"Missed you, bud." She smiled at the child gnawing on his cracker and fist.

Ginny slid the teacup in front of her. "I hope you had a better time than you look."

"I had a fantastic time. The problem is, either I have jetlag, or I've brought a traveling bug home with me." Picking up the teacup, she stared at Freddy. "I thought I would be feeling better by now. Should I leave in case Freddy or you catch it?" she asked worriedly.

Taking a sip of the tea, Alanna felt the effects from it immediately. She jumped off the chair and ran into Ginny's guest bathroom.

After barfing up what she felt was her left kidney, she was finally able to wash her face and splash cool water over the back of her neck.

Ginny was waiting outside the door sympathetically. "I put Freddy down for an early nap. Are you okay?"

"I feel like I'll survive now. It must have been something I ate last night."

Ginny gave her a pensive look. "Could you be pregnant?"

"No, there isn't a chance of that being possible."

"Do you know how many have thought the same thing, only to find out they are?"

Ginny walked closer to her, so Alanna was forced to take a step back inside the bathroom. She watched as Ginny opened the small closet and reached inside a basket to take out a thin box.

"Here. I have a couple of extra pregnancy tests left over from before I became pregnant."

Alanna started shaking her head. "There's really no way. I've never even had a period ..."

"Then you're probably not. The good thing is, it doesn't hurt to take the test." Setting the test down on the sink, Ginny went to the door. "I'll give you your privacy. Just call out if you need me," she said, closing the door.

Staring at the test, Alanna started to open the door again. "This is ridiculous. I'm not pregnant." She looked at the test. "This is crazy."

She rolled her eyes at herself for even thinking about taking it. Nevertheless, her hand went out to pick the test up.

"What could it hurt?" Ginny would have proof she wasn't, and she wouldn't have to explain there was no way possible she was pregnant.

She took the test, then washed her hands and sat on the side of the tub to wait. Passing the time, she looked through different Crock-Pot recipes to broaden her horizons. Matthew loved spicy ... She glanced over at the test, blinked at seeing a line. What did that mean?

Belatedly, she scanned the instructions. She had to blink again. She was still staring at the test in her hand when Ginny gave a soft knock before entering.

"Well?"

Alanna turned the test so Ginny could see. "This can't be right."

Ginny gave her a mischievous smile as she reached back into the small basket. "Luckily for you, I bought in bulk. Can you go again?"

Numbly, she nodded.

"Cool. Then I'll leave you again."

Alanna stared at the closed door.

This time reading the instructions carefully, she took the test again. She washed her hands as she stared at the test carefully, not taking her eyes off it, as if a little gremlin had switched the last test to pull a sick joke on her.

When the test came back the same way the first one had, she picked it up, as if it would change just from her touch.

Swallowing hard, she opened the door. Expecting Ginny to be there, she went in search for her in the living room. But when she entered the room, she saw Matthew sitting with his hands in his lap. He must have left his shop in such a rush because he was still wearing the gloves he used when he worked in the forge.

Hearing her enter the room, he lifted his head. From the hopeful look in his eyes, Ginny must have told him what she was doing in the bathroom.

"We shouldn't get our hopes up until I go to the doctor's office to get another test," she said huskily.

"Does it say you're pregnant?"

She nodded in dismay. "This can't be accurate, Matthew. I've seen several doctors who told me it's impossible for me to become pregnant."

He nodded back at her. "Then we won't get our hopes up until we know for sure. I'll call—"

Ginny cleared her throat from the kitchen. "I just called my obstetrician. She's going to work you into her schedule." Ginny went to a glass tray beside the door. "Here, you can take my car."

Removing his gloves, he handed them to Ginny then took the car keys. "Ready?"

Bemused, she followed him to Ginny's car.

The whole way to town, neither of them spoke. After parking, Matthew was out of the car and opening her door before she could even unbuckle her seat belt.

"There's no way, Matthew." She tearfully took his hand.

"Alanna, I'm going to love you the same way I love you now, when we go in that door, as when we come out."

Gathering her courage, she was already preparing herself to feel the bitter pang of disappointment until she looked up into his face. He was smiling down at her with the full wealth of the love he felt for her.

Gripping his hand tighter, she pulled it to her cheek, feeling the soothing warmth that never failed to calm her.

"Fire isn't your gift."

"It is—"

"No, being able to start a fire is just a part of you. Your true gift is how you make people feel, how you make me feel."

"How do I make you feel?" he asked hoarsely.

She could answer him with one simple word.

"Loved."

Alanna looked up from watching the tiny hand clutching her finger at the sound of the bedroom door being opened.

Smiling at Matthew as he walked inside the room, she then frowned at seeing the pale complexion on his face, which wasn't there when he had left to get her suitcase from his truck.

"Did we forget something at the hospital? There's no need to be upset if we did."

"No. I forgot the suitcase. I'll go get it in a minute. I was just talking to Silas." Matthew sat down on the side of the bed, where she was lying with their newborn son.

"Did he want to come in to see the baby? I don't mind—"

"No, he left. He'll come back later."

"Matthew, you're scaring me ..."

Matthew was terrible at hiding his feelings, and she could see anguish plainly in his eyes.

"What's wrong?" she asked fearfully.

"Greer had a stroke."

"Oh God ..." She sat up in the bed. "How bad is it?"

"Bad," Matthew told her, his face twisted in grief. "He had it three days ago."

"Three days ..." Her voice broke off. She had been in labor three days ago. Their eyes met, thinking the same awful thought. She started getting off the bed.

"Is he still in the hospital?"

"No. They just brought him home. He refused to stay there any longer. What are you doing?" he asked, gently lifting the baby into his arms.

"Getting dressed. You're taking me to see Greer."

Tate answered when she knocked on Greer's door. Lines of fatigue fanned across the man's face as he stared at Matthew then her questioningly.

"May we see Greer?"

"Greer isn't up for visitors. He just got home from the hospital."

She didn't move away from the door, pleading, "We won't be long, I promise."

Tate moved away from the doorway, allowing them entry. "Greer won't want to see you. He even locked Holly out of the bedroom."

Entering the home, she saw Greer's other brother, Dustin, and Greer's wife standing in front of a door. Both turned as they approached.

Dustin gave Tate an irritated glance. "I told you to get a screwdriver, not to let company in."

Tate shrugged. "They can't do any worse than we're doing. He's been locked in there for an hour."

Alanna stared at them in shock. "You haven't busted down the door? What if he's had another stroke?"

Dustin and Tate stared her down.

"I hear him throwing stuff. He just doesn't want us to see him. Besides, I just came back inside from looking through the window. He flipped me off."

"In that case." Alanna moved away from the door. "Open the door, Matthew."

"What makes you—"

"If you can open a cell door, you can open this one."

Matthew gave her a harassed look.

"He's not in the best mood for company ..." Dustin warned.

Alanna twisted her hands together. "I just need to ..." Blinking back tears, she tried to get out what she wanted to say and couldn't.

Matthew swore under his breath, moving his hand to his pocket. Taking out his pocketknife, he opened the blade and slide it into the metal lock, then shimmied the knife until the lock clicked open.

Quietly opening the door, she went inside to see Greer sitting in the darkened bedroom, staring out the window. The bright sun from the window allowed her to see where to walk to him sitting in a wheelchair.

"Go aw-away," he said in a thickened voice, turning from the window to stare up at her.

Greer's ravaged face had her going to her knees. Unable to hold back the tears any longer, she burst into sobs.

Laying her head on his lap, she cried so hard that she couldn't stop pouring out the anguish she felt at what had happened to Greer. The cocky man who had driven her nuts in jail and who had almost destroyed her wedding dinner by getting into an argument with the caterer, and pretty much anytime she and Matthew grilled out, was the former shell of the man he had been when she had seen him last; which was when he gave them a police escort to the hospital when she went into labor.

A heavy hand landed on her head. "Qu ... it. I can't te ... ll which one of u ... s is wett ... ing my paj ... amas."

"You're paying the price of me having a baby ... I wasn't meant to ..." she hiccupped.

When they had come out of the doctor's office with her

pregnancy confirmed, she still hadn't believed it possible. Matthew had sat in the car and explained about Greer's healing power, which was a secret their family kept hidden. They had come to the conclusion that Greer must have healed her when he held her bandaged hand, inevitably healing her womb.

"You may have just been trying to heal my hand ... but you gave me so much more, Greer." She lifted her eyes to his. "You gave me a miracle." Turning her upper body, she held out her arms to Matthew, who had come in behind her and gently gave her their child.

Holding her son, she turned back to Greer to place him on Greer's lap, so the baby was lying longways, letting Greer get a good look at what he had made possible.

"We named him Greer Alexander Coleman," she told him softly. "Greer after you, of course, then Alexander after Alexander the Great. We"—Alanna had to push back another sob—"named him after men who don't have the word *defeat* in their vocabulary. You made me whole again ... Greer. Matthew may have brought the sun back into my life again ... but, Greer, the gift you shared with me ... made the impossible ... possible. I should be the one paying ... not you."

Greer's face twisted as he tried to form words.

"Don't ... stress yourself." Wiping her tears away, she gave him a firm look. "So, this is what I'm going to do. Every day, I'm going to come over and bring little Greer Alexander with me, and I'll work with you on your speech. Then I will help you with your physical therapy exercises."

Instead of looking pleased, Greer started shaking his head. "Do ... n't need yer hel ... p."

Standing up, she placed her hands on her hips. "Holly and I will go over your menu, so you're only eating the healthiest foods, which will help you regain the strength you need. No more fatty steaks, fries, triple decker burgers."

Greer's eyes started to bug out when she mentioned the triple decker burgers.

"You're going to be back on your feet like this." She snapped her fingers, which resulted in her waking baby Greer. She let the baby cry for a couple of seconds before lifting him into her arms to pass him back to Matthew, who was manfully trying not to laugh, while Dustin and Tate had to leave the doorway when they couldn't hold their laughter back.

"Oh ... and before I forget, I'll have Matthew take down those 'No Trespassing' signs that read 'you're dead in sixty seconds' to 'you're dead in ten minutes, give or take' until you get the hang of running again."

She turned to look at Matthew, who was putting baby Greer back in his carrier. "Did I forget anything?"

"No," Matthew said before he couldn't hold his laughter any longer at Greer's affronted expression.

Turning back to Greer, she gave him one more tidbit to chew on. She reached out to smooth his white hair down then placed a hand on each side of his face. "By the way, don't think you're going to keep that door locked. Holly looked pretty upset when I got here. We don't want her worried about you, do we? Take it from me, Greer, she doesn't give a damn what you look like. I guarantee she's just thanking God you're alive." Straightening, she moved away from Greer. "See you tomorrow. Rest up."

She breezily left the room and went around the corner to find Dustin, Tate, and Holly waiting with admiration on their faces.

She opened her mouth to say something, but Tate put a finger over his lips, motioning for them to go outside.

On the porch, Tate double-checked to make sure the door was closed before doubling over.

"You know that cut Greer to the soul about his signs, right?"

Her lips twitched. "Matthew did mention how serious he takes his signs."

"No one touches his signs." Dustin snickered, having to brace his weight against Tate. "Then you threatened to take his food away. Jesus ... I bet, when we go back in, he begs us to take him back to the hospital."

Alanna curled her arm though Matthew's, happy their spirits had been lifted and they didn't seem so dire as they had been. Maybe a small part of Matthew's gift was rubbing off on her.

"No, he won't. He's gotta prove who's greater ..." Holly gurgled with laughter, wiping her tears away. "Him or Alexander."

Her expression grew serious. "Thank you for coming by. You gave Greer something to worry about more than his recuperation. Before you came, he was worried if he would be able to talk again. Now I think he's more worried about whether I'll ever let him eat steak again. The only thing Greer loves more than talking is eating."

Alanna shot Matthew a teasing glance. "I thought on his wavelength."

"We should be going." Matthew gave her a broad grin then looked toward the sky. A brewing storm cloud was moving closer.

Telling the Porters good evening and promising to return tomorrow, they hurried to the truck, wanting to get the baby inside before it started raining.

Heading back to the Coleman's side of the mountain, Alanna turned to stare at Matthew's profile as he drove, thinking about how much she loved him and the family who she had grown to adore. She had the family she never dreamed was possible.

She turned her head on the headrest. "Let's stop by Silas' before going home."

"Alanna, you should be in bed, resting."

"I want to check in with Silas. I know how close he and Greer are. We won't stay long."

Matthew made the turn into the long driveway, and as they pulled in, they saw Ezra sitting in the grass, staring up at the darkening sky. It had become a familiar sight over the eleven months since she had lived here.

She waited for Matthew to open her door and help her down. Then, standing by the front of the truck, she looked up at the clouds, which were growing darker by the minute.

She heard Matthew coming to her side after getting Greer out of the truck.

"I used to hate clouds when I saw them in the sky. I felt as if they had it out for me, just waiting to weather one storm after another alone."

Matthew hooked an arm around her shoulders. "You don't feel that way anymore?"

"No. I have you and *our* family to weather any storm with me." She moved her eyes to Ezra, who had been sitting out, watching the stars more often. Also, every time she came across the brothers lately, they would talk in hushed tones. Something was coming, and they were preparing for it.

She worried it concerned Kate, who had convinced the authorities that she wasn't involved in Elizabeth and Owen's plans then promptly disappeared.

Alanna gave an internal sigh. She didn't know if Kate was the looming threat Ezra was watching for, but what she did know was that you couldn't predict a lightning strike. You could only make sure you were not out in the open. The Coleman brothers provided that shield. They had the courage to take the storm, knowing the sun would come out again.

How could they not win? she thought, staring at her husband with his love for her shining in his eyes. They had the sun as their secret weapon.

"I remember the best advice I've ever been given. When I look up at the clouds, I say two little words."

"What words?" Matthew gave her a curious smile.

"Fuck 'em."

Afterword

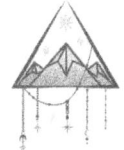

Mother stepped out onto her private balcony to read the stars. They were growing dimmer with each millennium that passed. The faith that was all the gods' lifeblood was becoming extinct. The heavens depended on the mortals' devotion, just as much as the mortals needed the gods' favor.

The heavens and the mortal world had come to a crossroad. One wrong turn, and a darkness never known before would envelope both worlds, bringing an end to both.

Gazing at the mortal world, Mother refused to shed the tears stinging her eyes. He knew the cost he would have to pay, yet he had healed that which wasn't meant to be healed. Through his interference, a life had been created, a life which had not been meant to be.

She stayed her hand from removing his gift, yet his punishment was not done. He must learn his lesson and learn it well. The female child needed his guidance. She must learn the cost of her gift, and only he could teach her the gravity of the decisions she would have to make one day. Even then, Mother didn't know if it would be enough to prepare her.

Pinpointing the star she was looking for, she finally allowed herself to shed the tears she had been holding at bay.

Truth be told, she would never admit it, but she wasn't as angry at him as she should be ... Had it been anyone else, his mortal days would be over, and he would be trying to appease her anger in person.

Still ...

Mother dried her tears. The brief storm over. He must learn his lesson. She couldn't have him upending her plans for her warriors.

Veering her gaze slightly to the stars that represented her warriors, she examined the sky like a chessboard as she placed her emotions aside and resumed planning her next move.

What to do ...? What to do ...? Mother mused. *Aha.*

A knight is always ready to jump into the fray ...